An Angel For Lisa

For Marian
2002
Our Love
Jim & Diane

An Angel For Lisa

Diane Ashley

Writers Club Press
New York Lincoln Shanghai

An Angel For Lisa

All Rights Reserved © 2002 by Diane Ashley

No part of this book may be reproduced or transmitted in any form or by any means, graphic, electronic, or mechanical, including photocopying, recording, taping, or by any information storage retrieval system, without the written permission of the publisher.

Writers Club Press
an imprint of iUniverse, Inc.

For information address:
iUniverse, Inc.
2021 Pine Lake Road, Suite 100
Lincoln, NE 68512
www.iuniverse.com

Any resemblance to actual people and events is purely coincidental. This is a work of fiction.

ISBN: 0-595-25353-9 (pbk)
ISBN: 0-595-65117-8 (cloth)

Printed in the United States of America

To my beloved husband,

Jim

List of Main Characters and Dates

(*Bible Quotes: Good News Bible—Today's English Version) Important dates of reference:
May 10, 1964————Sunday—Cassy & Lisa's birthdays

September 29, 1984————Saturday—John & Lisa's wedding

December 30, 1984————Sunday—Alex is born

February 3, 1988————Wednesday—both Cassy's accident & the twins birth
* Note: 3 hours difference between Eastern and Pacific time!
May 17, 1991————Friday—John Elliot Mason born

List of Characters for reference:
Cassandra Lee Elliot-Cassy
Parents:
Lee Ward Elliot
Lynne Reily Elliot
Friend:
Nancy Susan Panaé

'Mason Haven'
John William Mason
Wife:
Lisa Anne Myers Mason
Children:
Alexander Windsor Mason
Cecilia Lynne Mason
William Brett Mason
John Elliot Mason
John's Parents:
William Shay Mason-Bill
Marcela Benson Mason-Marcy
Friend & Manager:
Amos James Hardy
Doctor:
Dr. Aaron K. Simon

'Windsor Stock Farm'
Mr. & Mrs. Franklin Murry Windsor
Son:
Frank M. Windsor
Farm Manager:
Jebadiah Louis Myers-Jeb
Grace Anne Myers
Daughter:
Lisa Anne Myers
Friend: Sally Marie Jones

CHAPTER 1

"And now these three remain: Faith, Hope & Love, the greatest of these is love."

I am Lee Elliot. During my life on earth I was Lynne's husband, and Cassy's father. Now I am a soul in the spirit world, and feel as if I am father to both Cassy and Lisa. From this perspective time does not exist. Therefore I see their lives all at once. Human emotions remain, and for this reason I ache for them and love them both. Knowing what will happen makes me want to help them, to change many things. Of course I cannot do this. But it comforts me to know there is a way to rescue Lisa. Perhaps sharing their stories with others will ease my thoughts. Their stories could help people traveling life's journey. It may serve as a warning against all that is evil in human behavior. If sharing helps one soul, or eases their pain, it will be worth telling.

When human suffering becomes entangled, so complicated, intervention could become necessary. Lives may bond together as with Cassy and Lisa. Two young women, born the same day and year.

They come from totally different worlds, and will become closer than twin sisters. We are unaware when angels carry out the will of God in help of human souls.

It is my tribute to them, in telling their stories. We all know humanity is full of folly, and racially prejudiced views. This is invalid in the face of God, and with unconditional love. First I will share Cassy's early life, and what leads up to the bonding of Cassy and Lisa. Then of Lisa's growing up, and her young adulthood. Later, a more detailed account of their soul to body joining when it actually takes place. Also an unfolding of what life holds beyond. More important, how Cassy and Lisa's lives are forever intertwined and fulfilled. After all, it's not the gifts we are given in life that count as much as what we choose to do with them!

On May 10, 1964 not long after Lynne's husband died, she was born. Her mother named her Cassandra Lee Elliot, after her father Lee. From Cassandra came her nickname of Cassy very early on. The name fit, and it stuck with everyone. Her mother Lynne started it when she was a baby. Lynne soon left the mid west, and the farm belt behind. Her heart broken, she took Cassy to New York where she had grown up. There were cousins and friends living there that gave a sense of family. All her growing up, and married life they'd been poor, and scratched for a living. They had no money for luxuries, now on a waitress' salary nothing had changed. Cassy was the joy of her life. When she was seven years old and could understand, Lynne told her about her father Lee, and how he died.

Late one Sunday evening Lynne sat down with Cassy to tell her.

"Sweetheart, in the early years of my marriage your father and I were migrant farm workers."

"What's a migrant farm worker?"

"It just means we worked very hard picking food for other people, and we moved a lot. Wherever work was, we traveled to that farm to make enough money to live on. When we knew you were coming, we both wondered how we could best take care of you. We needed to do another kind of work so you could go to school regularly."

"I love school, especially reading and writing. When the teacher reads to us it's such fun. She's reading us *Charlottes Web* right now."

"That's a very good story Cassy, I've always liked it too! Now, let me finish please. One reason your daddy and I were working extra hard was to earn the money to move to a house. We both wanted to stay in one place so you could grow up with the same friends."

"Oh, where did my daddy live when he was a little boy momma?"

"His parents, your grandma and grandpa Elliot did the same, they lived in the mid west and worked in crop picking and he helped them. He had to move many times and didn't get to go to school every day like you do. We wanted your life to be different, better."

"One day he was severely hurt in the spring harvest close to the time I was due to deliver you. The doctors and nurses tried to save him, but he died during surgery honey. He went home to heaven to live with God."

"Can daddy see us now momma? Does he know what we do and say?"

"Hmm, that's a very good question young lady. I'm not sure, but it is possible because God can do anything! There is one thing I am sure of."

"What?" (Cassy listened excitedly to all Lynne's stories of her father and their younger days.)

"Your daddy is as proud of you as I am and loves you very much. Now it's time to get to bed, tomorrow is a school day."

Yes, from time to time, they did have normal mother daughter arguments. Over all however they were extremely close. Their love carried them through those rough teen years, and late curfews, that are always stressful. Two women in a home tends to result in some edgy, down right cranky times…In addition it was doubly hard for both not having a husband and father in their home. Still, the loss drew them toward being a strong team. Besides, they were good friends.

When Cassy was older, she started working to earn extra money. As young as ten, she began baby-sitting. At fifteen she waited tables at the same café as Lynne. Both dreamed of college for her. They saved what they could for sharp name brand clothes, and books. She graduated from high school early at sixteen with all A's. She qualified to take a test putting her into college for the fall semester.

Over the summer, she worked two jobs, one as a girl Friday in a law office. Then at night, she worked as a cocktail waitress in a hot nightclub where tips were great but she hated it. Men stared at her, and tried to grope her from behind. Yet, it was a means to further her education. One night a man pressed her against the counter close as possible. His breath was nasty and sour. He whispered near her ear:

"What time ya get off baby?"

'You scum,' she thought jamming her heel down hard into the top of his foot! With a forced smile, through gritted teeth she said,

"Why do you ask, SIR!" He got the message, and left the bar within minutes.

'Oh yes' Cassy thought, 'I'm becoming very good at foiling these attempts!'

'I'm no beauty even though my figure is at least average, or better. My hair is neither thick nor thin, and according to mom, it is just the shade of my father's. A shiny light auburn that sun streaks in the summer. My eyes are hazel like moms, nice eyes but not all that special with ordinary face features.' This is how she saw herself, as an ordinary person. Lynne thought her daughter was gorgeous! She did well in college and enjoyed New York State University completing her BA degree in Business Administration, with English, as her minor. She graduated Phi Beta Kappa, when she was only twenty years old. Lynne was so proud of her. Cassy promised herself she would help her mother when she had a good job. 'Perhaps I can help purchase a home for her retirement, and supplement her social security, it won't be much even after many years.'

One evening before bed, they relaxed each enjoying a bowl of cereal Lynne switched off the television. Glancing over, she said,

"There are so many things I never had the opportunity to do. I want your life to be different. It's my dream that you'll always follow your heart, take risks, make a place for yourself in this world."

"Ahh Mom, you know I'll rip up the streets to do that! We've both worked too hard not to succeed, you know I'll go for it."

"As for me," Lynne said sighing, "I want to stay in New York, perhaps move up state or even better somewhere on Long Island after retiring."

Her first choice was a place on or near the coast. The ocean brought her peace, and reminded her of her youth, and growing up. For as long as she could remember the very smell of the surf was as a lover beckoning. Like the call of home, it had a familiar fragrance, and comfort. She wanted her daughter to know this security too and to feel it deep within as she did.

During her senior year, Cassy sent out resumes to several law firms on the West Coast. She was excited with anticipation. One of her professors was from the San Francisco area and familiar with the different firms. She heard from three by the end of the year. During spring break, she flew out for an interview with the prestigious *Brown Brown and Taylor*. They hired her on the spot. Soon after graduation, she began work for them as an executive assistant.

CHAPTER 2

Nancy Panaé, Cassy's dearest grade school and college friend also moved west. Like Cassy she already had a job secured. Hers was executive secretary for a successful accounting firm. They planned all through college to room together on the West Coast. It also allowed Nancy to be closer to her relatives in Oregon. Rooming together was fun, a kick for them both. They rented half of an older two-story duplex, decorating it upbeat and trendy. Each had plenty of room, both were comfortable. Besides, since they were such good friends it worked like a clock, they ticked along together on shopping forays, supper, dating, and side trips. It was a little like college, but more fun, without homework, and exams! Near the end of their first year there, Cassy received a note from her mom.

"Hey, Nancy listen to this, it's a letter from my mom."

'Dearest Cassy, Finally your mother is retired! With my savings, I was able to buy a small cottage I love, with affordable payments. Best of all, it is within walking distance of my beloved Atlantic Ocean. I can't wait for you to see it; I'm looking forward to Christmas. Cassy, I am so happy here, what a blessing it is to have this new found freedom. I've included my full address and phone number here in Berry Cove. Directions are detailed below; it's easy to find. Give my love to Nancy, and wish her a Merry Christmas. See you soon. All My Love Mom'

Nancy went off to Oregon to be with her family, Lynne, and Cassy spent the holiday together on Long Island at *Berry Cove,* New York. As soon as Cassy arrived she took one look and loved it.

"I love your home mom, it's weather beaten siding, complete with freshly painted shutters. You've certainly found yourself a doll house."

They walked the sandy beaches together knowing this was special, an island in time. Though the weather was frigid, they bundled up and collected a variety of seashells, one to put a marine biologist to shame! They decorated the shelves among Lynne's books, arranging them artistically together.

"I'm so happy we have this time to spend together. This is a pretty generous Christmas bonus after just one year don't you think Mom?"

"Yes it is, and I'm so happy for your success Cassy. So proud of you honey, I always have been. You've accomplished so much in such a short time. You've fulfilled so many of my dreams for you."

"Thanks and I have you to thank for most of it, without your help I never would have done this well. We did it together."

Lynne snuggled deeper into the chair she was sitting in saying,

"I haven't been this happy in I don't know when."

"A Christmas to remember," Cassy hollered as she snooped in the refrigerator for a snack pulling out an orange.

After coffee the next morning, Lynne said, "I know what let's do, we'll get the tree today, and after supper decorate the whole place."

"That's a great idea Mom."

They had so much fun; the smell of pine and cookies filled the small house. Talk was free flowing and full of nostalgia as they bantered back and forth baking and even made a batch of saltwater taffy. It stuck like glue wherever it touched.

"The peppermint tastes great," Cassy said as they sampled, and laughed at each other's faces.

Later as Cassy looked around the sitting room she said,

"Your curtains are gorgeous, they look great with the antique furniture. The whole home is full of your special touches. Oh my gosh, where did you find that old desk?" With a broad smile Lynne answered,

"I splurged when I saw it in the second hand store, isn't it perfect?"

"Fabulous" Cassy said!—Both admitted it was the perfect touch for the room along with the over stuffed couch and chairs. Uncluttered warmth, just the look Lynne loved.

On Christmas Eve, they went to a candle light service at the small church Lynne attended. Afterward sipping tea by the lighted tree Cassy shared one of her deepest yearnings.

"Some day, I'd really love to have children of my own, that is when I meet the right guy." Almost immediately she lost the smile that had been there, just a second ago. Lynne quickly replied,

"You know, your father and I were blessed to be lovers, as well as best friends. I so wish the same for you. By the way, how is dating coming along, have you met anyone special?" She knew the answer, but couldn't resist asking.

"No Mom, she said with a smile, no one yet, at least that I'd date more than once, or twice."

Time passed quickly, and before they knew it, they were on their way to the airport. They were just in time for Cassy to catch her flight back to San Francisco. Before waving goodbye, Lynne hugged her close, and held on tight. "I love you so much Cassy," she kissed her cheeks, and tears welled in both their eyes.

"I'll come back on my next vacation, hopefully this coming summer," Cassy said.

"Just try and stop me, you know I love you too,—Bye Momma."

At the same instant they both thought: 'I haven't called her that in ages Cassy thought!' And Lynne: 'Gosh, she hasn't called me that in ages!' Indeed this was a golden moment.

It was a smooth uneventful flight back. Nancy was there early to pick her up. Soon as she saw her she yelled, "Hi, how was Christmas?" Cassy raised her voice above the crowd, "Great, just wait till you see the cool house my mom found! I hope you'll fly back with me, if we can get time off together on our next vacation."

"It'd sure be fun," Nancy said, "Let's find your luggage and grab a burger, are you hungry?"

"I'm starved Nan, and I want to hear about your holiday too."

CHAPTER 3

Wednesday February 3, 1988 San Francisco California and Meade Kentucky

It was 6:00 AM. Cassy left early for work. She had a heavier than normal workload today. She hurried, grabbing her keys and purse as she ran out the door. Smiling she thought, 'as usual I'm leaving without any breakfast, old habits die hard after all these years.' Coffee was enough for her, the cup at home and more at work hot and black. 'I'll more than make up for it at lunch, and dinner,' she thought.

Traffic was heavy as she pulled onto the expressway heading toward the office. She was head executive assistant for a young lawyer, Brian. The truth was Cassy did a lot of work, probably more than Brian. He was an up and coming corporate lawyer with several large accounts in the firm of *Brown, Brown, and Taylor*, he being the son of Edward Brown. Brian was undefeated so far in his first three years, and more than proud of it.

Since her college days, Cassy's life had been relatively dull by most standards. Sure, she had dated a few men, but none had knocked her socks off. In reality, some dates were down right boring in a funny way. A fact she shared with Nancy to their mutual delight. For instance her last date, she met through friends at a dinner party. It was their first and last. All he did was talk about football the entire evening. When fed up, she smiled sweetly and asked him,

"Have you ever played quarterback?" Just to see if he was listening.

"Why yes!" He said.

Still smiling, with wide eyed innocence she quipped,

"Ever made a forward pass to a girl?"

With an earnest puzzled look he said,

"Yeah sure, but she wasn't there to catch it!"

"Hmmm," she said,

"Can't imagine why not, it must have been incomplete!"

She and Nancy nearly laughed themselves silly over that one. 'What a dumb sports jock he was!'

Then there was Nancy's favorite date. A guy named Tom, who droned on all evening about how great he was, how his boss said he was the most intelligent employee he'd ever had.

"A promotion is eminent," he said! As Nancy yawned he woke her up with a question.

"How would you like to pay for your dinner tonight, cash, or credit card?" Yes, and if that weren't enough to set her teeth on edge, he then asked if she would like to come up to his place for a cozy night cap. To that invitation she replied,

"No thank you Tom, this may seem odd to you, but I'm not in one of my cozy moods." That date was worse than Cassy's jock, but they laughed at poor deluded Tom too.

It is now about 6:15 AM as Cassy heads for the Bay Bridge musing to herself, 'all my dates leave me with an empty feeling. There hasn't been one man who has captured my heart, or love. Brian is a handsome man in a way, if you're attracted to mannequin perfect features. He hasn't shown any interest in me, though we're together nearly every day. Besides, there's a regular parade of women in and out of his office.' She made up her mind sometime ago to return the compliment. Thus she let him know subtly, she was immune to his arrogant assumed charm. He must have felt rejected, or ego driven, for he asked her out to a non-business lunch last week. She emphatically declined, and Brian appeared to be moping! Secretly Cassy admitted to herself that this pleased her greatly! She'd begun to long for a day or two away from the city. She used to love hearing the stories her mother told about the freshness of country air. For all the work involved, even the taint of sadness didn't deter her thoughts. Fantasy tinged her daydreams about meeting a special man. It sounded good, escaping from smog, and the hassles at the office.

Reaching over she clicked on the cassette player, and adjusted the volume to hear her current favorite, *Phantom of the Opera*. Closed up in the car, there was freedom to enjoy it loud enough to drown out most traffic noise. The mellow voice of Michael Crawford, was a perfect contrast to Sarah Brightman's soprano. The music soothed her soul, there was never a time that listening didn't give her chills. Thoughts of the heart shaped and reshaped within her mind. When the show came to the theater, she and Nancy bought tickets. They both loved it, and each had a copy of the sound track. 'Hmmm traffic seems heavier,' she thought. Idly her mind wandered in daydreams knowing they would increase as spring approached.

"Shameful," Cassy said aloud to herself with a secret smile of delight.

She was driving in the lane nearest the rail, when she heard an air horn blowing behind her. Without warning, a car cut off a cement truck, forcing it into the right lane. It slammed into the rear of Cassy's car with tremendous force. The truck shoved Cassy's car through the bridge railing; it plunged toward the water and certain death far below. It was winter, a typical damp foggy San Francisco day. The Pacific Ocean was rough, white caps foaming the surface blown by strong winds. Visibility was poor, hampering any rescue efforts. Police had their hands full rerouting traffic, and closing the bridge. The repair work would take time even if the crew began today. Right now, the police had reports to take, and the press was already having a field day.

There is something macabre about how people gawk at the scene of any accident. They practically line up for interviews. As the drama unfolded one officer said, "do you think these fools believe they will make the six o'clock news?"

The fire captain he spoke to said, "Who knows, it's the same everywhere we go!"

'Just human nature I suppose,' the officer thought to himself.

In spite of the seat belt, she was wearing; her head smashed with terrible force into the windshield. Cassy never felt the water's force because the impact knocked her unconscious. Up above, sirens blared as police and ambulance made their way to the scene of the accident. The one car and driver that didn't stop was the one who cut off the cement truck. They slowly continued off the bridge with the other drivers under police direction no one the wiser. It happened so fast that apparently no one noticed his or her license plate number. No one ever came forward with it. Odd, how life simply continues routinely for those citizens not directly involved in the drama of an accident or tragedy.

Several people stopped to help, more just to gawk. The cab of the cement truck teetered over the edge of the hole in the bridge. People were screaming and scurrying around. Someone tried to help the driver to safety before the emergency crew arrived. Miraculously the driver lived, suffering only a broken leg. The police called the coast guard, to notify them of the accident. A television crew from KNCT arrived to do a live broadcast. News as it happens, that's their motto, money the driving force!

Water seeped into the car faster and faster. All the while Cassy was unaware of her present life slipping away.

I am frantic at this point as Cassy's father. Time passed indeterminable, into a space and realm where only God knew what was to be. An angel of the Lord is speaking to Lee of Lisa in Kentucky.

"Lisa's journey on earth is finished; her dear soul is complete, and needs rest. Cassy's body has been in an accident, which should not have been. Her soul's journey is not finished—she must go back. Lisa has a small baby boy, and—twins coming! They must have a mother, the right mother."

Then the Lord God said,

"Send Cassandra back to finish her journey of life in Lisa's body, as Lisa's soul returns home to me."

The angel speaks again,

"She will fulfill Lisa's life as wife, and mother. Now I must prepare Cassandra, help her understand this new life she will fill."

Cassy's father speaks to the angel.

"Please, can she see me, may I speak with my child? I couldn't be there when she was born, or help her mother. I missed out on so much."

The Angel answered,

"No, she must not see you! However you will see her, be with me in her presence when I speak to her. She will feel your love warming her, making her feel secure. You will hold her! It will be God's strength through us for His glory."

Spiritually cradled in her father's arms, Cassy was comforted. She felt as if she just woke from a good night's sleep. Strangely, fear never entered her thoughts in this invisible world of the spiritual. Instead, a feeling of total contentment and sheer bliss swept over her soul. She slowly began to wonder where she was, and what had happened. Instantly the answer came as light to her eyes. A benevolent presence told her that she was safe, she'd been in an accident, all is well. 'Will my Mother be okay?' Again the answer came, 'Yes, she will be all right and comforted.'

In San Francisco this is how Lynne and Nancy coped with the tragedy of Cassy's death. It took until the following Friday before the weather cleared enough so they could locate Cassy's car with her body still inside. The little vehicle had drifted from the location of the accident further complicating the recovery. They had to use a barge with a crane to retrieve it. By then Lynne was there from *Berry Cove,* she and Nancy claimed the body and made all the arrangements. There were so many details to tend to with reports and interviews. They decided to have her funeral locally, but Lynne wanted her body buried at the cemetery in New York. She didn't understand why, but it felt right. Lynne was grateful Nancy was there. She didn't know what she would have done without her. Not since the death of Lee her husband had she felt so shattered, broken, and alone. Day by day she would survive, having Nancy was a tremendous comfort. She was hurt too losing her best friend. They cried together, went through it all. A lifetime of close friendship developed between them.

Meanwhile in the spiritual world I was still with Cassy. She was held fast to a dream of vivid color warmth and rebirth. A strong loving voice firmly told her she must return.

"Your life is not complete! Your journey is for another one born the same day as you, she needs you desperately. Her life must ebb away; the need is very great! All you need to know will be given you. All you need to learn you will learn. Grace will be given to you. Trust my child!" In this dream state, in total comfort she waited until…It was time for her to return to earth, to new life, rebirth in abundance.

She is at peace. As her father, I am filled with joy. 'Odd how humanity lacks the ability to grasp the fullness of eternity with our loved ones. What a gift life is, with its turns and changes without warning. The Almighty had it well in hand when He created our souls for eternity.'

In *Meade* Kentucky at 9:15 AM the rest of the human drama was taking place. Life and death holds four souls in balance, Cassy, Lisa, and the twins. Soon a miracle will happen. We in the spiritual realm wait for this bonding of body and soul: Several seconds passed, then finally success! Sighs of relief follow then a cheer in the operating room. Lisa's vitals begin to stabilize. Now is the time, the instant of the miracle! The change came in the blink of an eye; both Cassy and Lisa are fine.—As her father Lee Elliot, I am ecstatic for her new life in Lisa's body! Lisa's soul is at peace with us, safe in the spirit world. Now I will tell of Lisa's growing up, young life, adulthood, and what the future holds.

CHAPTER 4

North Georgia Windsor Stock Farm 1974 Lisa's Story, Growing Up
"Cruelty shrinks the spirit, Kindness expands it, And love, Like no other balm heals it" Ada

Frank Windsor held his sour smelly hand over Lisa's small face as he forced his way into her tiny squirming body and savagely raped her.

She was nine years old.

"No—!"—"Stop plea-se, let me go!" Her muffled screams went unheard.

That day Frank took more than Lisa's innocence and virginity. He took away her chance for a normal life. He blemished her future; caused her terrible pain and terror deep within her psyche and soul. This was the first time he raped her, but would not be the last.

As he raped Lisa, sweating and grunting like a pig, he coarsely whispered, "You tell anyone, bitch...and I'll kill your mother, and that is a promise."

Lisa was terrified and believed Frank would kill her too, if she told anyone. That night as she lay in bed her body trembled and shook on the inside...It would not stop. She thought, 'I feel filthy dirty. There was blood on my panties too. I'm dirty like they are.' Early the next morning Lisa took her panties out into the field behind her home. She buried them as deep in the red Georgia clay as she could dig. She spent a long time scrubbing every day until her skin was nearly raw from soap. She continued this extreme daily ritual of washing. Nobody seemed to notice the extra washing. Lisa didn't understand why she never felt clean no matter how much she bathed.

In pre civil war days, *Windsor Stock Farm* was a large powerful cotton plantation worked by many slaves. Lisa's ancestors remained after the slaves were set free. The early Windsor families were as fair and kind, as they knew how to be, and paid what they could afford. Windsor was the only name or home known by them.

There certainly was a mix of blood in Lisa's heritage. From her mother's side came African American, and Caucasian. Her father was African American, American Indian, and Caucasian. All of these culture clashes formed a most beautiful, though troubled child. Her hair was beautiful; it was curly and thick like a loosely braided rope. Lisa preferred wearing it this way keeping her hair out of works way. Her skin was a marvelous creamy bronze color. Through out the county, those folks who knew her casually, or just saw her pass by guessed she was perhaps Italian, or Spanish.

Lisa learned the ugly side of life at an early age and frantically did her best to avoid Frank Windsor when ever possible. Her understandable hate and fear of him bordered on paranoia. Her mother, Grace worked in the main house cooking and in general ran the place for the kind, and elderly senior Windsor's. Her father, Jeb was assistant manager and stable boss. There were times when Frank, as manager, interfered. He seemed adept at causing trouble and made bad business decisions. However, Frank spent much of his time chasing after Lisa, Sally, and other girls.

Sally was Lisa's closest friend at Windsor, and another victim of rape when the only thing she should have known was how to help make lemonade. Sally was an orphan, and a year older than Lisa was. She was huskier, and full of fight and spunk. Frank thought of Sally as a challenge as she grew stronger. Even in his vile drunken stupor's he knew time was short. Sally would soon be too old and of little interest to him. The two girls never talked about their dark secret. Sally suspected that Frank bothered Lisa, but she wasn't sure. This also fueled Sally's hatred, Lisa was like a younger sister to her. Lately she would sometimes see Lisa alone under the shelter of a moss-laden tree. She would hold and hug her stomach and rock it, as if holding on would give her comfort.

Frank Windsor had complete control and used it to his advantage. His idea of fun was a bottle of whiskey and forcible rape. Frank was a greedy predator of the worst kind. He preferred children, young female children. Lisa's gentle shy ways made her more vulnerable to his filthiness. He made sure when he banged her head it hit her scalp where it would not show.

Today the pride of Windsor farm is their huge stock of Thoroughbred horses. One real joy in Lisa's life are the horses. She is an expert at gentling the foals, when not helping her mother at the main house. Her father taught her to ride when she was barely old enough to walk. Love came natural, no teaching necessary. Lisa loved helping her father train the little ones. Her parents were loving and attentive whenever they could be. However they worked very hard long hours. They did not know about the obscenity that continued to terrorize their young daughter.

CHAPTER 5

About nine years after Lisa was raped the first time she began to feel sick in the mornings. She couldn't keep much down, and she lost weight. Her mother explained long ago about her periods, so when Lisa missed she suspected what was happening. Frank raped Lisa at every opportunity. Still she kept it to herself, and prayed. Oh how she prayed for God to let her die. She felt shame although she was blameless. If she had to live, she hoped and prayed for a little boy baby. Lisa believed he would be safe from Frank.

They were expecting business guests the following week at *Windsor Stock Farm*. Friends of the family, Bill Mason, and his son John from *Mason Haven*. The Masons also bred and trained Thoroughbreds. In the horse breeding circles of Kentucky, the Masons have the finest reputation. They sent a request to Windsor for the purchase of a stud, and brood mares, with a date set for arrival. They arrived in their truck, and a new air-conditioned horse van. It was an impressive looking rig and the Mason's were very proud of it. To give comfort to their horses was an added joy for everyone at *Mason Haven*.

Looking around the place John remarked, "Damn but this is a massive estate dad."

"Yeah!" Bill said, "you should have seen it in the old days. Your grandfather used to bring me here! Those pillars on the old house nearly always had a fresh coat of paint as well as the barns, and out buildings. Horses, man they must a had near a thousand head, and they still raised some cotton then too."

"Well, it still looks good to me," John said. Just then, one of the stablemen came running over to show them where to park along side the barn in the shade.

Lisa and Jeb were working a few of the foals.

"It's high time these younguns are halter broke to lead," he said with a smile. Lisa warmly returned his smile, she was proud of her dad. Jeb bent over picking up a soft cotton rope that fell from the fence. John saw Lisa as she gazed at the foals with softness in her eyes.

Although Lisa was pregnant, it did not show. She was quite a sight in her boots, jeans, and pale green shirt. John didn't miss anything, not a bend or a curve of her slim hips, or full breasts. Her dark eyes and beauty had him riveted! She was turned sideways with her arms around a bay filly scratching her ears. In one easy move she slid the rope halter up and over her head speaking softly.

John was mesmerized by the sight of her, and felt something indefinable in his gut. It was more than the obvious heat he felt in his loins. He felt a certain pulling, and tugging from deep down—in his heart? He pondered this as he asked,

"Who is she, Dad?"

"Why that's Jeb's daughter Lisa! My but she has grown since I was last here." John's eye's flashed,

"Well introduce me!".... Bill smiled nodding his head with a knowing look.

"Hey Jeb, I want you to meet my son, John. Who is that with you, this can't be little Lisa." Introductions were made around, and Lisa thought they seemed quite nice. She even thought John was…handsome!

As far as John was concerned, Lisa was the prettiest little gal he'd ever seen. Back in *Campbell County,* Kentucky John had a reputation for being a ladies man. He dated plenty of gals, but he never felt so physically attracted as right now. Yet there it was again, that tug, he had a durn soft feeling for this young Lisa.

That night they bunked in a guest room near the paddock. Bill wasn't surprised when his son, asked to stay behind to work the stud on the lunge line, and do extra training toward gentling him. He would take the mares back home and leave John here for a short spell. Bill thought, 'the easier the stud is to handle at home when breeding begins the better!'

John and Bill knew that Jeb had done a good job of green breaking him. He just needed those rough spots worked off. Bill also knew that John wanted the time to get to know Lisa!

He said, "Son I'll be back in a week or so to fetch you and the stud horse. I'm sure Jeb will let you use his pickup to get around while you're here."

"Great, Dad, if you're sure you won't need my help unloading?"

"Nah, Amos will be there to help son."

After visiting with Jeb, Grace, and Lisa, Bill paid his respects to the elder Windsor's at the main house. They had lunch together, and John met Frank Windsor. He took an instant dislike to him. Frank was surly and arrogant; he had been drinking heavily. After he wandered off, John said to his dad, "let's get those mares loaded, dang how can Frank be the son of these nice people?"

"Well, yep I reckon he is, though I agree you'd never guess it to meet him."

Bill said his good-byes to everyone within the hour and took off for home with the mares. John was already settled in and decided to saddle up one of the horses, thinking he'd look around the grounds.

Lisa was feeding and watering the horses. He walked into the cool of their newly built huge and sturdy barn.

"Man, but it sure is hot today," he said to nobody in particular....looking straight at Lisa. She gave him her best unconcerned look, and answered,

"Yes it is, Sir!" then went right back to the horses.

"Miss Lisa, which horse would you recommend?" It must have been a full two minutes before she answered.

"Well, why not saddle up that stud colt you're buyin?"

"Reckon I will" John said.

His dad told him the colt had rough edges. John knew he'd be in for a real duel the minute he laid eyes on him. He pawed the floor, and his eyes flashed white at the sides. He reared up and banged down hard and kicked the side of his loose box stall.

"Hmmm, Miss, I do believe you would enjoy watching me try to ride this here fella." The slightest smile crossed her face, and then it was gone.

"Why, John, Sir, I just thought you should get acquainted that's all" Lisa said.

John went into the tack room to grab a halter and lead, saying

"Think for today I'll just start him slow on the lunge line." Lisa didn't answer, but shadowed his moves, succeeding in not letting him know.

Just then, Frank walked in, Lisa felt cold chills from head to toe, and hurriedly threw a flake of hay in the last stall as she ran out with goose bumps on her arms.

"She sure left in a hurry," John said.

"Yeah that's the way with females, when ya want um ya gotta go get um." John thought to himself, 'what a crude bastard he is.' Frank offered to show John how to handle the stud saying, "ya gotta show um who's boss, rough-um up!"

"This horse is mine, and we don't train our horses that way."

"OK Mister," and Frank walked off saying he was making a big mistake!

John was invited to supper at the big house but graciously declined, thanking the senior Windsor's.

"It's been a long day, and I want to get started early tomorrow with the horse training." Sleep evaded John, he laid awake for hours thinking about what had happened. It really had been a long day. Just as he drifted off to sleep the image of Lisa came. She wore a tantalizing sweet smile as she floated across his mind…Her image remained!

CHAPTER 6

The days flew by. John talked to his dad, and knew he'd return in two days. The stud was beautiful, and a joy to work with. John began calling him Warrior the day after arriving—the name fit. He didn't see much of Lisa unless he went out of his way. She was busy helping both her mother and father.

One morning he spoke to Jeb asking if it would be all right with him if he invited Lisa out on a date.

"I'd like to take her out for supper and to see a movie."

"Fine with me son, but you'll have to ask her she's coming now!"

"Hi Lisa, if you're free tonight I'd like you to join me for supper and a movie, how bout it?"

"Well, I need to ask first, see if mom needs help."

"You're free girl, your mom and I will be fine tonight without-cha."

"Okay then, yes I'll go," Lisa said, giving him a bashful smile.

That night she wore a cotton sun dress in delicate lavender. He thought she was a vision, and her fragrance was even better. Lisa used a touch of *White Shoulders* cologne, a gift from her parents last Christmas. This touch of floral intermingled with her body's unique scent, and was irresistible.

John was on the quiet side himself, so being with Lisa was somewhat of a word challenge. However, she was easy to be with, her smiles warmed him. She was the quietest girl he'd ever been around. His words seemed to flow easily and being with her didn't make him feel uncomfortable. Lisa's mouth captivated him. He felt an almost uncontrollable urge to touch, to caress, and to kiss that mouth! All through supper, and all through the movie, this fantasy returned. Driving home down that long drive, John reached over to hold her hand. At first—Lisa felt an urge to pull away. At the same time, she wanted his hand on hers. A new and confusing experience for her. He was unaware that this was her first date with anyone. Lisa had been asked for dates when she was in high school, and also to the prom. She politely declined all invitations. Thoughts of boys, and dating understandably scared her, and made her feel nervous. Somehow John seemed less of a threat he was gentle.

Sliding out of the truck to get the door, He reached out taking her hand again. They walked to her home slow, without a sound. When they stopped at her front door, they turned to face each other. Lisa said, "Tha…" he softly put his finger to her lips silencing her. Looking into each other's eyes Lisa experienced her first real kiss.

She didn't expect this. John simply lowered his mouth to hers, just lightly brushing his lips to hers. He simply gave her a tender chaste kiss. This very gentleness made her feel weak-kneed and she yearned for something, but she didn't know what. It shattered her to the core. They parted, wishing each other a goodnight.

The next morning Lisa woke up feeling light-hearted for the first time in ages. That is, until she entered the kitchen and the smell of bacon hit her. She retreated fast for the bathroom retching and trying to be quiet. A cold washcloth on her hot face soothed her. Taking a deep breath, she tried it again breathing through her mouth. Grace looked at her as she came in,

"Honey you look pale, you okay?"

As Lisa pulled out the plates and silverware she said,

"Fine Momma,—really!"

The next day, Sally was helping Grace in the main house it was washday. Sheets would soon be hanging up all pristine and white. They blew like sails billowing in the breeze on the backyard clotheslines. All was peaceful and quiet on this clear warm morning as Lisa finished up with the horses. She'd soon be helping Sally and her mom—they'd be expecting her.

Jeb and John went into town for tack supplies. Saddle soap for one was in short supply. Bill would be arriving later in the day. The rest of Windsor's work crew were out in the orchards pruning trees, and cleaning up in general around the estate.

Lisa hummed as she went from stall to stall, watering and feeding oat grain mix to the horses. She loved this giant horse. She was there the night he was born. He was the darkest bay she'd ever seen, smart and quick too. Only in sunlight did highlights of chestnut show in his glossy coat. "Hi mister boy" she said, "How's Warrior today you're my big baby aren't cha." Lisa knew she should hurry and help her mom and Sally; still she loved to linger with him in the coolness of the barn. Of all the foals, he stood out in her mind as the best. She sure would miss him.

She started to turn when she heard an all too familiar slurred voice.

"He got cha all hot and bothered ready for me, look at the size a those testicles, n' that penis, near as fine as mine." Lisa's blood ran cold.

"No-oo, not again she pleaded leave me alone!" She ducked down, and backed away from Frank.

"Come over here to me bitch, ya can't get away," he croaked laughing. His evil laugh brought bile up her throat. It burned like fire.

"We're alone it's your chance to enjoy it, ya know ya want it."

Lisa concentrated on escape, but how could she. Warrior's loose box stall was in the middle of the barn.

"Come'n out-a there that horse ain't gonna stop me." Warrior sensing her nervousness began to pace. Lisa kept to the rear of the stall, as far away as possible.

"Aw right bitch Aw'm gettin ya now." Frank ducked under the nylon mesh barrier. Try as she did, she could not get away. He grabbed her arm even as she twisted vainly to escape.

The horse snorted wildly banging around with the two struggling people. Frank backed his elbow into his ribs, and Warrior reared up, coming down hard on his foot.

"Aa-oow you bastard horse."

Lisa took that second to jerk her arm free only to be caught again. This time he had her ankle and pulled hard enough to pull her off balance. She went down hard banging her head on the cement floor. She was sick and dizzy.

"Frank" she pleaded "leave me alone, I'm pregnant and sick let me go."

"So bitch he leered at her, ya carrin a Windsor huh, good aw own ya." Frank was pleased—he felt a sick sort of pride.

"I'm the stud around here!" He threw her against an open hay bale landing on top of her. Lisa could hardly breathe; it took the breath out of her.

"Go ahead" he said, "I like it when ya scream, no one'll hear ya." He had his pants down, and was now yanking on hers. He kept his knee planted firmly in her middle. Lisa knew intense hate in that moment through her pain. She struggled against him, as Frank thrust down and in claiming her body again.

He didn't hear Sally, as she came into the barn. She was insane with rage when she saw what he was doing to Lisa. Without a second thought, she grabbed the pitchfork and jammed it hard into Frank's lower back and buttocks. He screamed in agonizing pain, and was furious at being caught and interrupted.

He left Lisa to squirm and fight back her nausea. She tried pulling her pants up before she lost consciousness. Sally ran from him screaming.—He jerked his pants up, and dislodged the pitchfork that was stuck in his backside.

"I'll kill you." he bellowed. Sally was sane enough to be scared stiff. She knew her only chance to escape was out running him, or being heard.

When they pulled the truck in Jeb went into the house not hearing. However, John heard!

Sally continued screaming non-stop! When John rounded the barn door, he saw Lisa crumpled up in the hay. He ran head long past Sally, and squarely hit Frank in the belly with his head. They both fell to the floor, John yelled to Sally, "Call 911." She ran out of the barn to call.

Frank staggered up near the pitchfork, grabbed it and ran crookedly toward John.

"Come on!" John yelled, neatly side stepping the fork, and in one smooth move, kicked it out of his hand.

John was crazed with his anger and battered Frank with what ever he could find, they both fell again knocking a saddle off a rail. The saddle cushioned John's head.

"You bastard" Frank yelled at him. John jammed his fist into his face so hard he heard his nose crack, and break. Blood splattered everywhere at once. He fell backward, and sideways, smashing his head full force into one of the large steel support beams. Within moments sirens could be heard and people yelling, coming toward the barn. Frank never moved, his skull was crushed. Blood covered the barn floor all around the area where he laid. The sirens blared as three police cars and two ambulances pulled into the barn area.

John held Lisa in his lap rocking her knowing only her pain. The paramedics hurried to check her vitals. She was coming around as they waved an ammonia flask under her nose. While all this pandemonium went on, the police were swarming everywhere and calling the coroner's office. Bill Mason pulled in with the trailer rig.

CHAPTER 7

The coroner pronounced Frank Windsor dead at 11:20 AM and he was taken to the morgue. After the Paramedics treated Lisa, she was taken to *Mercy Medical Center* for diagnosis and further treatment. Grace and Jeb were understandably scared and followed close behind! They were terrified for her, and wondered how she felt. They wanted desperately to comfort her, to know her condition.

Meanwhile the police continued questioning and taking statements from John and Sally. While John answered questions, Bill sat near by hearing bits and pieces of what had taken place. He tried piecing together what had happened in his mind. John's thoughts were of Lisa, even as he continued answering the police. His mind raced, thinking, 'Dear God, what had that monster done to her beside the obvious? That she was frightened of Frank had been obvious before.'

'Damn!' He berated himself for not being there this morning to stop him. 'What if,—if only they hadn't gone into town' he brooded to himself.

"Huh?" John said, in reply to the officer's question.

"What time did you arrive here?" The officer was trying to be patient.

John said, "I'm sorry, I was thinking about Lisa! I'm not sure exactly what time it was, must have been shortly before eleven o'clock." Again, unbidden his mind screamed a prayer, 'please let her be all right.' He had no idea how badly she was hurt any more than her parents did.

'God what a mess this is,' Bill thought. Not knowing how long they'd be delayed he left the barn to call his wife Marcy. He walked to the main house to call where it would be quieter and more private. An officer was talking to the old couple on the porch. Both Mr. and Mrs. Windsor were crying. Though he felt numb with shock, Bill felt a stab of pity. He could tell the police were trying to spare them, and still stick to the truth, while doing their job. The *Beauford County Press* was there in full force. Most of the details would soon be public knowledge. In all Bill's years he'd never gotten used to how rude and invasive the press was. It seemed to him that some reporters actually enjoyed the questioning. The idea of asking how it felt to have your own loved ones hurt maimed, or killed appalled him! The very thought made him sick with anger, he sighed heavily.

Bill was so upset he dropped the receiver as he phoned. Pressing it to his ear he said, "Hello honey!"

"Hi you," she said.

"I have to tell you something important, try not to get upset."

"What happened" Marcy asked? All her senses were immediately impatient, and tense.

"I'm trying to tell you," he said exasperated.

"All right, I'm sorry I'm listening, go ahead."

"When I arrived here everything was in chaos. It seems the Windsor's son Frank attacked Jeb's daughter in the barn."

"What!" Marcy yelled, "You mean little Lisa?"

"Yes, it was Lisa! Apparently John came into the barn just after one of the other girls Sally, stuck a pitchfork into his backside. There was a struggle, a fight between Frank and John. Frank hit his head, and ended up dead somehow. It was and accident!"

Marcy screamed into the phone, "Holy shit, Bill, I want to talk to John!"

"I'm sorry, calm down, it'll be okay honey. You can't right now the police are still questioning him. I'll call back later and give you more information. Yes Marcy, he's not hurt all right! A few bruises is all, after he calms down he'll be fine. We'll both phone, and talk to you later. I'm going back to listen, and be with him now, goodbye love."

Marcy's head was spinning. She said, "Sorry! I just wish I was there, I should have gone with you, I love you, bye."

"There will be an inquest," one of the police officers said, "and more questioning later."

"Formal depositions will no doubt be taken, but the case seems open and shut." Bill over heard another officer say, "No arrests will be made today if at all. Much will depend on the out come of the autopsy." The police were still there by late afternoon taking statements, and gathering all the evidence they could. The Windsor farm remained in a state of chaos, and confusion as shadows lengthened into evening.

Although Lisa was awake in the ambulance she remained frozen in thought. Her mind raced backward, wondering about all that had taken place. Too much had occurred. She could not yet comprehend that Frank was out of her life forever. As she was wheeled into the emergency room, she wondered 'where's my momma, and daddy?' Tears stung her eyes; she desperately tried to cover her face up with her hands, but couldn't. Lisa was in a body brace, with an IV inserted and taped to her arm. The attendant tried to soothe her, "we're here in the ER now, you're going to be all right." She thought sarcastically to herself, 'yeah sure, and relax too I suppose, what do they know.'

The lights seemed too bright. The nurses were sympathetic and as gentle as possible. The ER doctor scanned the preliminary police report. It stated that she'd been raped. After examining her he asked,
"Did you know you're about three months pregnant?" She had no words to describe her feelings, and remained silent.
"Do you want to tell me what happened" he asked…. A long silence followed!
"Perhaps you will want to talk to someone later, it may help you feel better." Lisa thought, 'how the hell does he know, how I feel?'
The doctor said, "For now, you and your baby seem to be all right, are you having any cramping?" Silence,—she nodded no!
"All right young lady let's get you a room, and let your parents in to see you. They've been waiting, and are very worried about you. We're going to watch you closely for a few days, make sure all is well. From the MRI we ran, you have a slight concussion."

Jeb and Grace were finally allowed in as the nurse settled Lisa into a private room. As they came through the door, tears trailed down her cheeks. Sympathy always affected Lisa this way, touching her heart even more for the love shown.
"Baby, I'm so sorry," Grace said. Jeb moved over to the bed, taking her free hand in his saying nothing. He just looked into her eyes with so much love. Minutes passed, as he stroked her hair saying,
"Never again will he hurt you," the words came out with vehemence and passion!

Lisa cried harder thinking of the baby. Through her sobs, she asked, "Did they tell you?"

"About what?" both her parents asked together.

"I'm pregnant with Frank's child," she finally said.

"No they didn't sweetheart, perhaps they thought you'd want to tell us." She sobbed louder till her head ached and her shoulders shook.

"It's going to be all right now Lisa," her mom said.

"This answers questions we should have wondered about earlier. It's not your fault, none of it. We are both so sorry we didn't know, or realize what was happening. Somehow we would have stopped that monster. You look so tired; we'll go for a cup of coffee and let you sleep for a bit, try to rest now. The nurse said you need to heal, so at least try and relax." Lisa just nodded and closed her eyes.

Both Jeb and Grace felt drained with all that had happened. Heart sick for Lisa above all.

"Dear God Jeb, I can't believe we could have been so naive about what was happening right under our noses," she said as they walked to the cafeteria.

"I know, I should have known above anyone else and yes damn it, I feel guilty as hell." They sat in numb silence sipping their coffee. With much effort they were trying to absorb the fact that their Lisa was in fact pregnant, let alone sexually abused. 'Hell, the bastard raped her' Jeb thought.

"My chest aches with it Jeb I can't help it."

"We'll get through this honey, somehow we'll get through it, I love you Grace."

"I love you too," she answered.

Lisa thought, 'ouch my head hurts so bad, I wonder if I'm going to lose this baby? I hope I do!' Just for an instant these thoughts passed through her mind.

Then in complete conflict, 'how could I feel that way? This life is innocent of sin, I shouldn't even think that.' Reaching down with her one free arm, she cradled her softly rounded stomach. Just as she did a sharp pain gripped her uterus. She groped for the call button, and pressed it hard for the nurse.

CHAPTER 8

A team of nurses, and the ER doctor ran into her room. He barked orders like a drill sergeant.

"Add DES, 'Diethylstilbestrol' to her IV, we need to stop her contractions, elevate the foot of her bed immediately!" Lisa closed her eyes tight hardly comprehending what was happening. Jeb and Grace heard the code blue and recognized her room number. They were on the run to her. Just as they stepped inside a nurse said, "I'm sorry, you'll have to wait outside for now."

They examined her to see if there was any bleeding, there was. One of the nurses began packing her with gauze, and applied a pad. The doctor gave the ward nurse orders.

"Have a nurse stay with her for the next hour, then check her every half hour. Let me know if there is any change in her condition."

"Yes Doctor" she replied.

"What's going on?" John asked as he nearly ran into Jeb in the hall.

Grace looked at Jeb and nodded a silent message of permission to tell him.

"She's pregnant, and we suspect she is bleeding and may miscarry."

John was devastated, "God, it never crossed my mind she'd be pregnant, that S-O-B-!"

"Sorry Grace," he added.

"Never mind" she said, "that's exactly how we feel, the only good thing is, now he can't hurt her any more." Jeb leaned heavily against the wall, and said:

"Trouble is, there has been so much damage done and we suspect for much longer than we had any idea. It could take years, if she ever recovers from all he did to her."

'That is what will keep me awake at night' Jeb thought, 'I should have been able to protect her from this.'

Lisa's door opened as the nurses came out followed by the doctor. He explained to them that a nurse would be staying, and suggested they wait to see her for now.

"The bleeding seems under control, we should know within the next 24 hours if she will miscarry or not. Why don't you all go to the waiting room, it's only two doors away. One of the nurse's will come let you know when you can go back in to see her." John went back to Windsor's for the night.

Time passed slowly, as Lisa slept fitfully. When the long night was over she felt somewhat better physically. She would carry the baby to term after all. John waited until late the next day to see her, Lisa wouldn't talk. She turned toward the wall while tears streamed down her cheeks. He felt so bad for her, and so helpless. His feelings were mixed up, and he didn't understand them himself.

'Why,' he wondered 'do I feel so overly tied to her, responsible, deeper than I've felt for any other girl before-never before!'

The next day her doctor ordered a psychiatric exam for her, and a complete evaluation. He knew she needed counseling. They had a good rape-counseling program within the hospital.

The police decided there would be no further questioning of Lisa. The county recorder took depositions from John and Sally at the courthouse. They wanted a deposition from Lisa. However, when the report came in of how fragile her mental condition was, they waved it. With what the lab learned, and proved regarding Frank Windsor they had enough. In addition to the forensic testing, further evidence was not necessary. The inquest went routinely. Frank's death was ruled an accident. No arrests would be made.

Then the whole farm seemed to settle into a sort of business as usual denial of the entire nightmarish trouble. The media finally backed off, and even Sally went about her work in a quiet daze and worried more about Lisa's recovery than anything else. It seemed the death of Frank defused her usual hot-temper and rather cantankerous disposition. So with the exception of the senior Windsor's who in their deep sorrow and grief suffered greatly, life continued. The funeral caused them to lose their will for living. Frank was their only child. Oh but life, and its infernal routine wins out, as it always does.

Everything went along as usual. Salvation of sorts, in the mundane, work continues. Marcy and Bill spoke daily; she was eager to see both her men as soon as possible. It was all Bill could do to keep her there at *Meade* to over see the horses with Amos. There would be much catching up to do, when they arrived. John and Bill stayed on at Windsor's until after Lisa was released from the hospital. She seemed to respond to counseling over the week she remained for treatment. All signs of miscarriage ceased, and the ultrasound showed the baby was normal. On the surface, Lisa seemed better, though somewhat withdrawn. John visited each day but he was now feeling restless, anxious to go home with his dad to *Meade*.

Without further good byes, but with promises to keep in touch, they loaded Warrior into the trailer, and left for home. They hoped Warrior would add a few prize foals to sell to racing farms in future auctions. There were always farms looking for new blood to add to their string of horses. Indeed, Windsor's would have first pick of the foals thrown. Ol Jeb would choose well, he had a well-trained eye for good conformation in horseflesh. After all he bred and helped raise Warrior who had all the marks of a champion race stud.

As for Lisa it seemed the further her pregnancy advanced the quieter she became. Sally and Grace tried their best to draw her out with little results. At her last doctor's visit they did another ultrasound to determine the sex of the baby. It was clear Lisa would deliver a normal baby boy. Lisa decided to put an end to her counseling sessions. The psychiatrist wanted her on an anti-depressant but couldn't prescribe one safely until after the baby came.

The Mason's called each week inquiring and the answer was always the same, no change. The next week when Marcy phoned and talked to Grace, she had an idea.

"Let's see if Lisa would like to visit us for a while, perhaps a change of place, and being with Warrior again will lift her spirits. She can be with me, we can go into town to do some shopping, and I promise to watch over her Grace. Please talk it over with her and Jeb and get back to me, okay?"

"Yes I will, and thanks I am willing to do anything to lift this depression of hers, it's been awful lately."

Jeb called that evening saying they would drive up with Lisa the following week. He too was willing to try anything that might help her. With Lisa beginning her 6th month, they packed enough clothes for her stay, and left for *Meade* and the Mason's.

CHAPTER 9

The trees were beginning to turn, and there was a cold nip of autumn in the early morning air. They left Windsor, turning onto interstate 75 to make the drive from Georgia through Tennessee, to *Meade* Kentucky. The weather was threatening to storm with a heavy dark slate sky. Lisa stared blankly out the truck window lost in her own thoughts. Grace had her arm around her shoulder and cheerfully tried to encourage her to talk. She simply wasn't in the mood, so instead she engaged Jeb in some good old fashion bantering. Her teasing of him, of how forgetful he'd been lately caused a sardonic smile to cross his lips. Then he grinned at her weakly realizing her jibes were more an attempt to cheer Lisa than to tease him. Her withdrawal remained, and turned inward as she'd been since leaving the hospital a little over two months ago. There were few exceptions; this was her usual state of being. Sally cried this morning when they left hugging Lisa tight to her. Lisa remained dry eyed, but returned her hug telling her she loved her too, and would keep in touch by phone as Sally asked.

The drive always took a long, tiring, and full day, depending on how heavy the traffic was it could take longer. Time passed amiably if on the quiet side where Lisa was concerned. There were more stops for comfort with Lisa's condition demanding it. She needed the ladies room often, and was craving hot chocolate, sourdough toast and grape jelly today. Then she spotted a *Po Folk* restaurant and said, "hey Dad, please stop, I'm hungry for hot chicken soup, and maybe something else." Jeb grinned, "okay honey, we gotta feed you both, keep you and the little guy happy." It thrilled both of them to indulge her in what ever she wanted. Grace fussed over her and was happy to see her finally gain a little weight. Actually she asked for very little, she never had been a demanding child. Now a young woman, and pregnant, she was simply acting on instinct. Whatever her body craved, her mind asked for, as her hormones fluctuated and changed…

The closer they came to Kentucky, and *Campbell County*, the colder it became. Clouds loomed dark and heavy; it was raining hard now with flashes of lightening, thunder cracked so loud it hurt their ears. Before they left the interstate to turn toward the town of *Meade*, the rain turned to hail. It came down by the bucket full. The hail was the size of ripe summer cherries driven by forceful and ominous wind. The roads were slippery, and the hail made the ground look like it was wearing a blanket of early snow. By the time they pulled off the road and onto *Mason Haven's* drive, the shadows had long ago lengthened into darkness. The trees were hardly visible, just blowing silhouettes of black against the sky. Rain and intermittent hail continued to pound the earth making the landscape look like some sort of surreal painting on black velvet. In spite of the weather, or because of it, both Jeb and Grace felt happy to be there safe, and hopeful that this would be good for Lisa.

Marcy and Bill met them with welcoming smiles on their well-lit porch in the front yard. Bill helped Jeb in with their suitcases, and all their belongings. Marcy warmly hugged them both, and escorted Grace and Lisa into the living room by the fireplace.

"Can you believe this storm? It's more like winter than fall," Marcy commented.

"I agree," Grace said. "An electric storm always makes me jumpy and nervous when we're out on the road, we're mighty thankful to be here safe."

The men finished up. Both dogs milled around the front door with tails wagging. Seeing Tag who was of unknown ancestry served as a reminder to Bill and Marcy that John wasn't home. He followed him everywhere possible!

He wasn't home because he'd fallen back into his habit of going into town to have a few beers with the guys after the day's work. John had simply forgotten today was the day they would arrive. Marcy said nothing, but hoped he'd pull in any minute to join in welcoming them.

After a good hot meal everyone felt better, and Lisa asked how the horses were and when Warrior would be a daddy.

"Not too long, sometime in late spring, early summer. Several of the mares are expecting in late winter early spring, by two of our other studs," Bill smiled at her, pleased by her sincere interest.

"We hope you'll stay on as long as possible, and give us your advice with the young foals," Marcy added.

"Grace, you and Jeb come up and visit any time you like. We'll enjoy having your daughter's company, as well as her help. You will be invaluable when the foals arrive Lisa," Bill commented.

"Thanks very much," she said to Bill.

"You know Lisa, sometimes it's mighty lonely being the only woman around here." Marcy beamed at her. For the first time, they were treated to a genuine full smile from her. She was radiant in the living room firelight.

In *Meade*, after John spent the evening drinking, and flirting with Stella. They closed the bar feeling no pain. She invited him to her apartment, which didn't take much persuasion. He was definitely back into old habits. Stella had been his old flame in high school, and was always hanging around. It was obvious she was attracted to him. If the truth were known, neither was in love with the other. When John returned from college, she was working as barmaid at the local beer bar. *The Paddock,* is a regular hangout for most of the locals. John had a real weakness for that curvaceous body of hers, which she flaunted at every opportunity.

John pulled in at feeding time 5:00 AM. Direct to the barn he went, to help with the feeding of the horses. Tag caught up with him following along beating a staccato rhythm with his tail against his leg. Amos was already hard at work. Just as he rounded the corner into the barn Amos hollered at him.

"Hello Johnny, you been out all night, you young tomcat?"

"Yep he answered, and not feelin all that good either." Amos gave it to him, "O' and I'm a feelin sooo sorry for ya too."

"Thanks a heap" he answered.

"Did you forget Johnny, that Jeb, Grace, and Lisa were coming up from Windsor yesterday?"

He stopped dead silent in his tracks at that bit of news. He hesitated just long enough to gather his poor tired thoughts before exclaiming:

"Horse shit, I forgot all about it! Did mom or dad say anything to you about my not being home last night?"

"Not to me they didn't" Amos said, then added:

"But then I never talked to them at all, I ate at my own place last night. If I were you, I'd finish up here in a hurry and get on down to the main house." John thought that was a right smart idea, plus he was feeling more than a pinch of guilt about last night.

"Yeah Amos, I'm on my way, I'll see you later on today if I can get myself together. After I pay my respects to the family, I'm headin for my bunk for some shut eye." He said this with a weak smile on his tired dissipated face.

Just as he was walking into the house, they met him coming out. Grace and Jeb were ready to leave for home, and everyone else was out to say their good byes. The rain had stopped, but it was still over cast, damp and cold.

To say that John was embarrassed is putting it mildly. It was like getting caught with his pants down. He did his best to cover it up with a smile. Nervously and a little too loud he said,

"Sorry I wasn't home last night when you arrived. Have a safe drive Jeb and Grace. I'll be at home when you visit next time…I also hope it won't be too long before you can come, maybe you'll be able to stay longer." He couldn't bring himself to even look at Lisa so profound was his embarrassment. As they drove away, he stood behind his parents and Lisa. His mother had her arm around her, he thought she looked smaller than usual, and vulnerable. For John it was like watching an old black and white movie in slow motion. Unreal, as he stood there watching them wave. Feeling the fool, he lifted his arm too and waved at Jeb and Grace. They were already near the bend in the drive and probably didn't see him.

Bless her for knowing how to sum up any situation Marcy took charge.

"John, you look like you need some rest dear." He thought he detected a thick haze of sarcasm in her voice and knew he deserved it. She continued:

"Lisa and I have things to do, so we will see you at supper-six o'clock sharp! John groaned a sigh of inward relief, and a silent 'thanks mom.' He managed a

"Yes Ma'am!" As he hurried off to his own house down the road from the main home with Tag close on his heels.

Bill went off to tend to business with Amos and the rest of the work crew. Amos was their right hand man, filling in when ever they couldn't be there. He did a great job for them as assistant manager. Whatever was needed he tended to it, or saw it was done by the crew. There were ten, unless they hired on extra hands, and they all lived in either *Meade*, or nearby. Amos was thirty plus years old now, and was hired on as a young lad to groom and muck stalls. Some twenty-five years or so ago, they often referred to them as the glory days. Back then, and years before when Bill's parents were running the place. *Mason Haven* was not just a breeding farm, but a full racing and stock farm. Their racing silks were packed away now but the silk racing flag of silver and deep blue still flew proudly over the main barn. Originally there were more than one hundred acres of good Kentucky land purchased back at the turn of the century. Forty acres was enough now to manage with riding trails, nearly half in pasture, then paddocks, barns, out buildings and four homes, plus one guest house. The old racetrack was still in use to condition the yearlings and test their potential for sale. They even had a fair sized natural spring fed lake. It was tucked off in one corner of the estate, and they still keep it well stocked with fish. Whenever they could, Bill and Marcy used to pack a picnic and go fishing with John.

Every year they looked forward to spring and the new crop of foals. This year would be special with foals sired by their new stud Warrior. Mason's was strictly speaking a breeding farm with four studs including Warrior, and about a hundred brood mares. Marcy knew that Bill still missed seeing the Mason jockeys sporting their silks. She accepted it as he did the end of that era. The business had changed so much over the last forty years. Racing for the Mason's ended when Bill's parents retired and moved to Florida. They died when John was fifteen, leaving clear title to them. Marcy and Bill were both anxious to pass title to John and his future family one day. Retirement sounded good, after all their years of hard work. If only John would settle down and take on more responsibility. They loved the horses, and the farm but were now wanting time to spend together, relax and do a bit of traveling.

Each year Amos and the crew trimmed a whole pasture full of elm, and ash trees as well as maintenance work, grooming, and feeding the horses. Yearly they repeated the same obvious fact:
"Thank God we don't need to trim all the pine trees too."
John slept until just about time to feed the horses then he showed up to help with that. Bill worked on the books in the office; just off the den, a quiet room, well planned long ago. One thing that bothered Marcy and Bill, was John's lack of interest in bookkeeping. He was more than qualified to do them, but wasn't as adept at it as they were. John never liked keeping records; in fact he detested it preferring to be outdoors training the horses.

Supper went well, everyone seemed to have relaxed in spite of a busy day. Marcy and Lisa had managed to arrange her bedroom, and take a walk out to the main barn so she could catch a glimpse of Warrior. He definitely remembered her and she was thrilled to see him, though she had to move around more carefully being pregnant. Most of all, she would miss working and training horses until after her baby came.

The folks were relaxing around the fire when John glanced over at Lisa and asked,
"Lisa, would you like to go for a short walk, it's a beautiful night?" She stretched and yawned before answering him,

"Okay, sounds good just give me a minute to put on my coat and boots." It was truly a lovely night for a walk, the moon was full and leaves crunched under their feet while Tag tried his best to get Lisa's attention. It wasn't hard she reached down and stroked his silky head, his tail wagged like he was beating a drum. Lisa laughed; it was like music to John's ears.

"Is Tag always this happy?" Peaceful seconds passed between them before he answered:

"Usually, but he really has taken a liking to you Lisa. He doesn't take to everyone that way."

"I'm glad" she said, "I love all animals." Lisa giggled, "he's licking my hand!" Yes, it was a very good night for a walk.

CHAPTER 10

In retrospect, I think it was Warrior who made John aware of the depth of his feelings for Lisa; at least it began that way. She had only been at *Mason Haven* about a week, just long enough to settle into a routine. Lisa did as much work as possible to help Marcy. They also shopped together, and both enjoyed the others company. Marcy made sure appointments were set up with Lisa's approval with a new highly skilled OB-GYN doctor in *Meade*. She also talked to her and she agreed to go back for sessions of counseling. Today was her first session. It seemed to help and she really liked Dr. Simon.

It was late afternoon, time to feed the horses as John came into the barn. Lisa was enthralled with the newest batch of kittens. She fed them and their mother twice a day then played with them. Being involved, she didn't hear John or Tag come in from feeding the mares in the pasture. Tag was so used to the cats he ignored them completely. It was a picture to behold adorable fluffy bits of fur crawling all over her lap as she sat on a bale of hay petting and cuddling them. Warrior's box stall was just across from her and he kept up a steady nickering sound to get her attention. Every once in a while she'd say to him, "you big baby, I'll pet you in a minute." John thought to himself, 'my God that horse is jealous he doesn't have her complete attention! Well I don't blame him, I'd be jealous too. I've never seen her more radiant, or beautiful.' Tenderness filled his being, and he felt an adrenaline rush. His neck and face felt warm and flushed. Amos broke the spell coming in to help feed.

"Hello you two" he bellowed. Lisa jumped a little and then smiled at them both.

"When did you come in she asked?" They both said, "just now!"

As time passed, it seemed very natural to have Lisa there she fit in perfectly. Everyone seemed to love her sweet quiet ways. Whenever possible she walked daily. When Lisa walked after supper John made a point of going along, Tag trailed behind them, or sometimes bounded ahead if he smelled something interesting. Their conversation was easy flowing and relaxed, of the farm, horses, and Warrior in particular. They looked forward to the foaling season most of all. Some of the mares are due after the holiday time, others later on in the spring. The Masons have a top notch foaling barn. Both mares and foals are to live in comfort. All foals are registered as being born January 1st of the year they're born. It doesn't matter if they are born later in the spring. It gives them a good beginning toward a possible racing career!

This night as they walked silence stretched between them easy and natural. He was thinking how much she was like one of the family, a part of him. He also remembered their date back at Windsor's. There was that kiss…He'd never forgotten it and was relishing the memory now—oh that was sweet!

This evening as he walked her back to the house they lingered, then stopped. Without hesitation he kissed her ever so gently on the lips long and deeply as if searching for an answer from her. Looking into her eyes she seemed embarrassed or perhaps something more, something else.

"I'm sorry Lisa," he said, "I would never hurt you on purpose, or make you feel uncomfortable I just have an awful time resisting your mouth. You are beautiful. Do you know how pretty you are? I, I love you—I really love you, and I love your baby too. In fact I love every lovely part of you." Without looking up she flushed. Very quietly she said, "thank you John." That was all, nothing else. 'Was she dumb struck?' He wondered, if she'd heard him? John didn't miss a beat,

"Lisa, will you marry me?"

There it was out; he said it. This was what he'd been thinking about for days, not to mention the long nights. He felt better having said it, even if disappointed by her answer. John felt strange, and somewhat confused, more by—how much—he'd said, than by Lisa's reaction.

After what seemed like an eternity Lisa managed to say,

"John I will need some time to think about what you've said. I can't think right now. I will give you an answer soon." John wondered how soon—soon was!

"Time for you to go in then" he said.

"It's getting colder Lisa, and tomorrow comes early for me."

Two days have passed since John asked Lisa to marry him. It seemed that both were avoiding the other. There was a rainstorm later that night, which temporarily put an end to their walks. She wasn't in the barn when John came in to feed the horses with his rather large shadow Tag. Lisa deliberately went in earlier to feed the cats. Marcy and Bill's Spaniel had taken a liking to Lisa as well. And kept her company.

Neither Lisa, nor John had much to say, to each other or to anyone. Marcy and Bill felt the tension, knew something was wrong but they didn't know what it was. They were both very curious!

Then today, while putting towels away, Marcy went past Lisa's bedroom door. It wasn't closed all the way, and she caught a glimpse of her by the bed, what she saw touched her. Lisa was kneeling as a child, praying with tears wet on her cheeks. She left her alone going quietly past, putting the towels in the linen closet. Lisa was in complete turmoil; she cared about John but wasn't sure if she loved him. She prayed because it was the only way she knew to search out the answer. She kept asking herself what she was feeling for John, was it love? Her feelings were so mixed and confused by the awful things that happened to her at Windsor. Her pregnancy further complicated her emotions. It was nearly impossible for her to make a decision. Part of her wanted to marry him because her baby would have a good father. She also knew that wouldn't be fair to John. Over and over she wondered what would be expected of her as his wife. The fear of having sex completely terrified her, even with John as gentle as he always was.

Lisa was walking along the drive toward the main road, with Cookie beside her. The sun was out, and it was warm even in the shade. She was enjoying the fresh air and the beauty of fall as the trees changed to deeper shades of amber, plum, and rust. Marcy had a fire burning in their fireplace. Its acrid fragrance was one she loved, Lisa inhaled deeply and was rewarded by the smell of the sun-warmed earth, and leaves mixed with smoke.

'Gracious,' she thought, 'this extra weight I've gained is starting to tell on me.' Her breathing was somewhat heavier than when she left the house. Just then Lisa heard the sound of a vehicle coming; it sounded like it was coming from the road. Yes,—it was John coming in from somewhere. She felt like hiding but there was no where to go, besides it seemed ridiculous when she thought about it, he'd see

Cookie anyway. 'Sooner or later,' she thought, 'I need to give John an answer.'

He slowed the truck, and pulled up as he rolled down the window.

"Hi Lisa, how are you feeling? I've missed you, how about getting in with me; I want to show you a special place on *Mason Haven* it'll only take a little while, okay? Besides we need to talk."

Lisa had that look again, half way between shy and fear, 'OOPS he thought.'

"Give me a minute to climb in, I am getting a little tired." Before she'd taken three steps John was out and without preamble picked her up and sat her into the passenger seat. He got in, put the truck in gear and turned to the left at Mason crossing instead of toward the houses and barns.

'I wonder where he's taking me?' she thought but didn't ask.

Soon they were near a tree-lined lake; John slowed the truck and parked it by his old spot, where he'd caught most of the crappie, blue gill, and catfish. Right now that seemed so long ago to him.

"Sweetheart, this is my favorite place of all and I wanted you to see it. Sometimes it freezes in the winter and I used to slide all over it. One Christmas Amos was with me and we were both on my new sled sliding down that hill back there. Fast as we hit the ice we heard it start to crack. You've never seen any two guys move so fast in all your born days, it's funny now looking back. It isn't that deep but we didn't want to get wet either, it was COLD! The next year my folks gave me a new pair of skates, but that didn't last long, I outgrew them and always did prefer riding to nearly anything else. By the way, how do you think Warrior is shaping up?"

Lisa hesitated for a moment then said, "seems to me he gets better and more beautiful every day John. You've done a great job with his training."

John mumbled a sincere "thanks, please Lisa, don't you have an answer for me yet?" She nodded her head back and forth telling him no.

"I don't know what to say John you've been so good to me."

"Good to you! Lisa I want you to be my wife, I adore you there is nothing I won't do for you. Don't you know how I feel about you yet?"

There was a stretch of silence again. John continued trying his best to get through to her. His handsome face serious with an earnest expression of love. His blue eyes alone should be able to convey to her the depth of his feelings.

"Listen to me Lisa, I won't put any pressure on you as my wife. I want you to feel comfortable about our lives. We can be married as soon as you say, but I won't touch you until you want me to. Do you understand?" This time she nodded yes. But John wasn't finished.

"I know I'm not perfect, but will do my best to make both you and the baby happy. Damn it, he will be my son and no one else's. I want our lives as a family to be complete as possible." Lisa put her fingers to his mouth to quiet him. She gazed into his intense sincere face and was struck with the concern in his blue eyes. Lisa wasn't immune to John's passion, love, nor his rugged muscular male body. He was extremely handsome.

"John, I will be proud to be your wife, thanks for loving me, and for helping me understand." Silence again, she was lost in her own emotions that were full right now as tears began to flow down her cheeks. He tenderly wiped them away with his finger, then pressed his wet fingers to his lips; she took his hand in hers and kissed it. Then she reached up giving him a soft kiss, so soft on his lips. He took her gently into his arms kissing her—slowly, very slowly! Lisa was shy, but couldn't keep her hands out of his thick brown curly hair. This was her compulsion running her fingers through his unruly curls again and again. John knew keeping his promise wouldn't be easy, but he would keep it!

CHAPTER 11

That night supper was an occasion of celebration joy, and some concern. John asked Lisa to tell his folks the good news. She began, and John helped. He was too excited to keep quiet once Lisa began telling them. Marcy was happy for them. It was no secret to them that John was in love. They loved Lisa; however that didn't blind them to the strong likelihood that their marriage would have many lumps and bumps. They kept their personal reservations to themselves. Lisa was the woman their son chose! Bill went to the kitchen, and brought back a bottle of champagne to toast the young couple.

"Congratulations" he said, "we wish you both long lives over flowing with love and happiness. I've always wanted a daughter; both of us missed having a girl of our own. And soon we'll also have our first little grandson to love." Before long they were all on the phone to Jeb and Grace telling them the news. Their ideas, suggestions and names were needed to help plan the wedding. It was decided they would arrive two days ahead to fully enjoy the celebration. Jeb left the farm in the capable hands of a new assistant manager hired after Frank's death.

They didn't waste any time setting the wedding date only ten days away. First John went to their local parish in *Meade* where they attended church. He wanted to speak with Father O'Brien, make arrangements for their wedding day. He was delighted to do all he could to help make Lisa and John's wedding happy for them. They would celebrate their marriage in the beautiful sanctuary with lighted candles, to say their sacred vows to each other.

There was so much to do; a marriage application to file with the state of Kentucky. There were blood tests etceteras, and also inviting close friends and family members by telephone. They would be pressed for time as it was. Lisa's head was swimming with all the excitement, however she was happy, truly happy for the first time in years. They chose their wedding rings classic, and simple in style. Plain bands of gold except for Lisa's solitaire engagement ring which she proudly wore. In spite of the fast approaching date Lisa daydreamed. She thought about John, and the romantic aspects of the wedding its self. 'I didn't know a diamond sparkled this much. I feel special, and pretty,' happy thoughts as she gazed again at her engagement ring.

Sally would come with her parents. She couldn't get married without her life long friend. She would be maid of honor! John asked Amos to be his best man. And the men, they never seem to care what they wear as long as the tie isn't too tight!

Lisa would wear a comfortable not too—tight white velvet wedding gown and a full-length hand made lace veil. Her veil would have sprigs of entwined baby's breath, a girlhood dream. Grace, Marcy, and Sally went shopping with her to pick it out. They also chose their own dresses. Sally chose a shade of wintergreen for her gown. It was perfect; Lisa picked out lavender roses, and gardenias for their bouquets. They had a great day, choosing flowers, the cake, and then out to lunch, time just for the ladies. All were tired but happy! Sally kept saying how pretty they all were, and then added "me too"—followed by giggles. It was contagious, before long they were all laughing.

There was one little job John had to tend to in *Meade* that night at the *Paddock Bar*. He wasn't looking forward to telling Stella he was getting married. Just the idea made him squirm. He suspected she wouldn't be happy! Man alive was he right about that. He asked her to go outside for a minute to talk. It began all right with, "Stella, I wanted you to hear this from me instead of someone else." Then, "I am going to get married in a few days." Stella stood there silent in the semi-darkness. Even in the dim glow of neon light he could tell she was trembling with rage. He thought she was changing color too—getting brighter in the face and darker at the same time. She flushed from the rush of adrenaline. He'd never seen a woman that shade of red before. That part was rather fascinating!

"You son of a bitch" she spewed and raved on, "you bastard after all the time and years I've given to you. This is how you say thank-you and good-bye to me? You are nothing but a fucking bastard."

John wished he could disappear somewhere. He hadn't heard that many cuss words come from a woman's mouth before.

"Now Stella, calm down you knew I didn't love you, and you don't love me either. I thought we had an understanding that one day one of us would leave, and this is it for me. I won't be back, ever! I love this lady and that's just the way it is."

Stella seemed to grow a full two inches as she let loose with an exaggerated
"HA—!"

"Well you thought wrong, we had an unspoken bond between us. Trust me when I tell you this, you will be back! Never is a long time John and you will be back I promise you that. See you around!"

'Hmmm' John thought, 'if I ever want another beer I'll have to go to the *After Hours Club,* or the *Water Trough Tavern.*'

As John drove home it seemed to him that telling Stella was the longest half-hour of his life, and it actually only took about twenty minutes, maybe less. "Shit" he said, thinking, 'I never dreamed she'd be that bent out of shape about it.' He breathed a deep sigh of relief. 'Oh well, at least it's over and good riddance to her'—he thought!

The night before the wedding Sally and Lisa caught up on each others news and secrets. Late into the night they talked, Sally told her about Windsor's latest gossip.

"Remember Jim Landaus and Felicia Berl?" Lisa rolled her eyes and nodded, "I sure do, Felicia was always flirting with the guys that worked in the orchards. And Jim yep, he worked pretty hard but always had an eye open for one girl or another."

Sally added, "Neither one knew how to ogle without gawking, they were so dumb!" Muffled peels of laughter rang out. This laughter shared with Sally was just what Lisa needed to help her heal. The sessions with her psychiatrist were still grueling and difficult; her pain haunted her sleep and cut into her days.

Sally's laugh was infectious, they both had a case of giggles. Her eyes huge, her smile ear to ear as she obviously enjoyed telling Lisa about it.

"Felicia had the hots for him, and made sure to wear her lowest cut blouse and tightest pants whenever Jim was around. We ran into each other about two weeks ago, and she goes,

"What do you think about Jim, don't you think he's super good lookin?"

I just stared at her and said, "Yeah Felicia, go for him."

"Okay I admit it, I have no shame; it was a blast to watch them. I'm not sure which of them bested the other in their seduction. The flirting went on for weeks, and then one night I was taking out the trash and saw them. There was just enough moonlight combined with the yard lights. They were as close as two pancakes could get standing up against the barn. I figured they'd finally decided to try each other out, or at least to wear out each others lips." Both Sally and Lisa covered their mouths to muffle more hysterical laughter.

Lisa asked Sally how the Windsor's were getting along these days.

"I never blamed them," Lisa said. "I knew they had no idea what an awful man their son was. I was so stupid not to tell someone, anyone!"

"Well, I didn't either" Sally said, "and I am older than you." Her eyes were bright with unshed tears. Lisa made a face that conveyed she understood. "I agree, we should have told and remember too well how disgustingly repulsive and cruel Frank was. What a relief he's gone!" This was one subject neither would ever laugh about.

"Lisa you may already know this, your parents told the Windsor's about your baby being Frank's child. They feel terrible that he hurt both of us, and any others that he may have molested. They realize he was very sick and wish they had known ahead of time," Sally sighed. "Both expressed the hope of being able to see your baby one day, but know you've been through enough. They don't want to add to your pain, otherwise they are getting along all right." Lisa stared blankly at her feet; "I don't want to hurt them either. We'll share the baby with them when we can, they're his grandparents too."

Lisa woke early that morning and immediately felt jittery and anxious. She looked over at Sally sleeping in the other bed and felt better just having her there. A smile crossed her face as the baby stirred and kicked. It felt like a new miracle each time he moved. She marveled with each flutter, and wondered what her baby would look like. She hoped—then stopped, 'NO—I won't even think about it.' Lisa couldn't help hoping the baby wouldn't resemble or remind her of Frank Windsor.

'This is my wedding day' she thought, 'and tonight I'll be Mrs. John William Mason!' As she was thinking how good it sounded a gentle tap repeated on the bedroom door. Sally rolled over and moaned, mumbling "no not yet, it's too early."

"Come in" Lisa said knowing it was Marcy, her Mom, or both. The house was still quiet but you could feel the excitement in the air.

Marcy brought in a tray with orange juice, toast, and hot coffee for the girls.

"You are spoiling us," they said almost in unison. Sally was sitting up now rubbing her eyes, and smiling.

"Good Morning you two, relax and enjoy your breakfast. I figured this would be plenty for now with the wedding at noon and the buffet after you will have tons to eat then." Lisa's first thought was she wouldn't be very hungry, she still remembered morning sickness!

"It's 9:00 o'clock Lisa, we'll give you and Sally till 10:00 to get your girl stuff done and then its time for us moms to have fun helping you get dressed for the wedding. The photographer will be here at 11:15 for a few pictures at home, and then we'll need to beat it over to church."

It was September 29, 1984 a perfect autumn day, with the sun shining, and the air crisp. The flowers, buffet and cake were ready; all was in waiting at the decorated church, no hint of any problems ahead. John booked their honeymoon at bed and breakfasts all across the lower east end of Kentucky and back home again. He also chose what he hoped was the perfect wedding gift for Lisa. A new pale blue Chevrolet Malibu which was being kept hidden till after the wedding. He figured sight seeing would be the best for her, certainly nothing more strenuous than walking planned.

John smiled to himself thinking 'it will be fun to drive, after all it needs breaking in and she shouldn't be driving too much. Maybe just enough to let her get the feel of it, after all it's her gift!' Thoughts came to mind of perhaps another trip later on after the baby is born and she is feeling better.' He knew from what his mom said that women feel better when they get out of maternity clothes. John was brought back to reality with his dad's knock on the front door of his house. Without waiting Bill came in.

"Hey Sonny, it's time for you to get dressed for the wedding, pictures in twenty minutes."

"Okay, I'll be out soon I'm almost ready." As his dad left he felt a flutter of something in the pit of his stomach. A reminder that he was more than nervous today. For just a few seconds he wondered what the heck he was getting himself into.

CHAPTER 12

The ladies came in one vehicle and the men in another. Grace was commenting to Marcy how relieved she was that the buffet would be catered. For once she wasn't responsible for either the cooking, planning, or its clean up. After parking the car they all assembled in the bride's room, which was off to the side of the vestibule. More than a convenience was the attached restroom, an absolute necessity! It seemed as though Lisa had just left the bathroom at home.

"Gotta go," she said, as she headed for the door. Sally followed on her heels to hold the skirt up for her. For some reason that amused them both and they started laughing again. Both Grace, and Marcy joined in thinking it looked funny with Sally at the side holding up the full heavy velvet dress.

The wedding party was comparably small, and that helped make things run smoother in spite of the hoopla. They all arrived at about the same time each to fulfill their roles for the wedding. Jeb and Amos would begin at the back of the church for obvious reasons- Sally as maid of honor, and Amos as best man, and the father of the bride escorts his daughter down the aisle! However for now all the men were assembled outside near the side rear entrance of the church. Jeb and Amos still smoked and so they stood out there visiting and enjoying their cigarettes. The side door opened and Father O'Brien joined them.

"Hello he said, are you ready for this wedding, how about it John?" He felt anything but ready at the moment but grinned saying,

"Ready as I'll ever get!" The priest grinned back and said,

"Y'all have about five more minutes before it's time to be inside." When he opened the door they could hear the organist warming up the keys playing favorite songs of both Lisa and John's, *The First Time Ever I saw Your Face* and *Only You*. Before long she would be playing the traditional wedding march.

At about that same time, a woman's voice could be heard above the din of talk, and organ playing.

"Jebadiah and Amos, hurry please, it's time for you to be at the front of the church with Lisa and Sally!" It seemed Grace appointed herself wedding coordinator, unofficially of course!

Earlier in the week when the Mason wedding announcement appeared in the local paper the *Meade Sentinel,* Stella found it. She'd been checking every day watching for it and smiled inwardly, it wasn't a happy smile but one with a plan. She read it over several times as images of how she could ruin things, and make John as uncomfortable as possible formed in her mind.

Stella Anders pulled into the church parking lot after everyone else arrived, with just enough time to sneak in and sit where she figured John would see her first, before he saw his bride! That was her plan anyway not to disrupt the service exactly but to stay long enough to unnerve him. A special little reminder from her to him letting him know she was still there. Stella was like an evil spider all dressed in bright red sitting in her lair. A flamboyant sight with her bleached blond hair! So far nobody knew there was an uninvited guest in there presence-'so to speak.' Despite the sun shinning, the church interior was sparsely lit aiding Stella with her plan.

All invited guests were there and seated ready for the wedding to begin. A young boy was lighting the candles on the altar, except for the unity candle in the center. From the back of the church Lisa and her dad could see into the sanctuary through the windows in the swing doors. Then one of the ushers pushed the doors back and propped them open as the organ began playing the traditional version of *Ave Maria*. Amos with Sally on his arm started walking forward. Lisa kissed her dad's cheek. She whispered:

"I love you, you will always be my best man." They both felt their emotions teetering on the brink but held them in check. Just as they began their walk down the aisle he said, "Lisa, you're a grown woman; I've never seen you more beautiful. We adore you, your mother and I are so proud of you."

Up front on the right John rocked on his feet slightly back and forth looking past Amos and Sally for a glimpse of Lisa and Jeb. However instead he saw Stella in all her gaudy array. The instant he saw her their eyes locked. Her trip was rewarded by the look of horror on John's face. There was nothing he could do about it and she knew it. John did his best to concentrate on Lisa's face and the sweet beauty he saw. The lunacy was in the contrast; Lisa dressed in white and Stella in glowing red. He swore inwardly at his own stupidity and wished this wasn't real. It certainly was a nightmare. His thoughts bordered on hysteria and minutes seemed like hours. Jeb and Lisa seemed to walk in slow motion, as in the movie *The Graduate* starring Dustin Hoffman, it crossed his mind and played in his head. He couldn't help thinking, 'what a paradox this is! Breathe John' he reminded himself. 'Take a breath, I am an idiot.'

At last Jeb and Lisa were in front of him, as thoughts of this moment became real and love washed over him like a baptism. Stella was gone, both from his mind and in actuality. The moment she knew she'd lost her hold she left. The rest of the ceremony was a blur for them both. Next thing he knew he'd slipped the ring on her finger that Amos expertly handed him. Their candle was burning and he vaguely heard the priest say, "You may kiss your bride."

Before the buffet was over, while holding hands, they went to each guest and thanked them. They lingered with their parents and also with Sally and Amos. Now it was time to surprise Lisa with her gift. Bill and John had it all planned the car was at the back of the church in an inconspicuous spot all decorated with flowers ribbons and of course tin cans! Lisa hadn't given any thought to what they'd leave in but if she had, it would have been John's truck. As Bill drove the new blue Chevy Malibu up in front her mouth fell open.

"Where did that new car come from she asked?" John simply smiled at her and said,

"It's my wedding gift to you Mrs. Mason." Lisa was truly overwhelmed. "I never dreamed of having my own car John, it's so beautiful, thank you." She put her arms around his neck and soundly kissed him.

"Thanks, thank you" she said again. Lisa couldn't stop her nervous giggle over her delight in this gift.

"Get in" he said, "our things are all packed and ready, let's go!" Having said their good-byes, and thank-yous, the newly married Mason's drove off. Their parents, with Sally and Amos stood there waving with thoughts of good luck and wishes of happiness in their minds.

CHAPTER 13

*L*ate September in Kentucky is an awesome sight. Change from summer to fall is dramatic. Nature was putting on its show; everything seemed iridescent after a brief rain. The late afternoon sun was reflected through all the bright color. Lisa was taking it all in as John drove; he glanced over and smiled to see the look on her face. They were on highway 80 in Boone National forest heading toward Salsville to stay the night. The next day they'd head for Buckhorn Lake and spend a couple days there.

"John, I think Georgia is pretty too, but the change is not as colorful as here, its' drier, and the bushes and grass turn brown in the autumn. Here the trees turn all these super bright colors!" He was enjoying the new car and savored it before answering.

"It's probably because Kentucky is quite a bit further north, our winter here will be colder too. What did you think of your new car when you drove it, did it handle smoothly?"

"Actually I don't know how to answer that John, I only drove it a few miles after we stopped for gas before you took over again, I do love the way it smells though! Maybe if I drive it again I can get a better feel of it." She smiled sweetly at him, and looked sideways to see if he knew she was teasing him. He didn't catch it to her delight, and he said,

"Yes, of course the next time we stop we can switch and you drive for a while if you want to,—if you feel up to it." Lisa laughed, and it sounded like fine crystal, with a musical ring, he loved the sound of it; it made him feel vital, more alive.

"What's so funny?" he asked. Lisa was enjoying this,

"I only laughed because I know you love driving, and I was just teasing you, although I would like to try it out again." It was John's turn to laugh now.

"You got me didn't you—you are a little minx!" Then they were both laughing and enjoying the ride.

Many miles away at *Mason Haven*, the two families gathered around a roaring fire talking about the day. They were all beat and tired, but felt content as they reminisced about the wedding. Both Marcy and Grace could hardly wait to see the photos. Jeb and Grace were planning to stay on two more days, and then they would head south with Sally, through Tennessee, and home to Georgia.

Amos and Sally visited at the church after the wedding. They made arrangements to go out that night after feeding the horses. Sally hurried in and changed clothes putting on jeans and a sweater to go to the barn. She liked Amos and his relaxed ways it made her feel good, relaxed too. He also told her earlier that she had a gorgeous smile! They tended to the horses, and other critters, assorted cats and John's dog, then headed for *Meade*. After the short drive they decided to make the rounds of a few local taverns.

They enjoyed a few beers, and Amos taught Sally to play pool. She played remarkably well for a beginner. They slow danced, and enjoyed the two step for awhile. Talk; that they did freely, and talked some more till late and now they were back home walking along the drive still talking. It was clear they were developing a good friendship. The playful bantering was fun for them; a well needed respite from work. When Amos walked her up to the door he wasn't sure if he should, but he wanted to kiss this lady. Sally helped him decide she didn't feel shy with Amos. She is however very short so she stood on her toes and leaned against him to reach his lips. She lightly touched his mouth with hers and whispered,

"Thanks Amos, it's been a very goodnight." He took it from there feeling on fire with the touch of her lips on his. They were wrapped tight in each other's arms. They said goodnight and it took a while!

Sallsville was a small mountain town, very picturesque. John pulled into the lot at the rugged looking, but charming bed and breakfast where they would spend their first night.

"Oh, it's beautiful here," Lisa said looking all around. John beamed at her, glad to see her happy reaction. After they were all settled in, they went down stairs to go out for dinner. He had reservations at the only nice restaurant in town. John ordered dinner with champagne, then canceled it when Lisa reminded him she couldn't have alcohol till after the baby came. Besides she said, "I'm not even twenty one yet!" They had seven-up instead. Lisa and John enjoyed themselves, and danced afterward. Both were laughing at how funny it was with her tummy gently rubbing between them. They had a live band playing slow standards, which was romantic.

The end of the evening went surprisingly well considering that John and Lisa would not be having sex till after the baby came. He showered first, and watched TV while she took her time doing all those mysterious girl things. He hollered in at her,

"Hey, I'd be more than happy to wash your back." She paused for a good long thirty seconds, before saying,

"Thanks John but I think it would be easier for us both if you didn't."

This time a smug smile crossed his face,

"I'm just teasing"—he said, 'aren't I,' he thought? 'Of course I'd be more than happy not only to wash her back, but all of her and then dry her off as well and then…. Well, it was your idea John!'

She came out timidly in a pale buff and peach colored negligee with matching gown, it contrasted perfect with her dark hair and bronze skin. She had brushed her hair, and it was hanging loose nearly to her waist. What a sight. John let his eyes feast on her. 'This is going to be harder than I thought' he mused to himself. With a smile he told her how really exquisite she was, the prettiest bride anyone had ever seen. She smiled back but still hesitated at the edge of their huge four poster bed. John extended his hand to hers saying,

"Come on Lisa, climb in here with me I won't bite." And that's how it was throughout their honeymoon. John kept his promise; he held her close, and kissed her gently but ardently, withholding all of the strongest passion he felt for her. Lisa was more than worth it to him; he loved her that much and more.

John thought, 'to quell my sexual appetite under these conditions would be near impossible for-any-healthy man. I'm proud of you John,' he told himself!

Lisa was happy, happier than she could ever remember. Being cuddled comforted, and loved in this way was exactly what she needed.

CHAPTER 14

"The words of the wicked are a deadly ambush, the wicked are over thrown and are no more."

A few days before their wedding, John and Lisa had moved her personal things into his home. There wasn't time before leaving on their honeymoon to put anything away. Everything was in disarray in fact it was hard to walk from one end of the living room to the other! The day after the wedding the family, Amos, and Sally all pitched in and moved things around. Now when the kids returned they could walk in and move stuff where they wanted it. Their wedding gifts were neatly stacked unopened in the spare bedroom. They were the only ones who could put their home in order. Jeb and Grace brought most of Lisa's remaining things with them, so those items were also sitting around.

There was a new television and stereo system which Bill and Marcy gave them. Jeb and Grace gave them a new bedroom set in traditional style. It was almost identical to the set Lisa had admired a year or so ago when they were shopping. Bill and Amos carried John's old bed and dresser to the storage shed.

Sally planned never to marry, so her gift to them was especially precious. She gave them her mother's set of classic gold-banded china. It was all packed carefully just as her mother had left it before her death of cancer some six plus years ago. Sally's father was a question mark. Her mom had been very candid about it. She told Sally that they met, had an affair and one day he just up and left her pregnant no good-byes! She sighed heavily whenever she thought about that. Sally figured that was as good a reason as any not to marry! Of course the whole tragedy of her rape at the hands of Frank Windsor added to the vehemence of her feelings. On an unconscious level, her rape was probably the stronger reason behind her wish not to marry.

When John and Lisa returned, and her parents and Sally were back home, life settled into a comfortable routine. Lisa loved having her own home. Together they put their home in order. She would arrange, and then rearrange the rooms while John worked. Fresh flowers were poking out of all their wedding vases. It was like playing house at first all things new and she loved it. One morning when the whole house shined like polished glass from all her scrubbing Lisa asked Marcy over for mid morning coffee and homemade cookies. They laughed and enjoyed each other's company. Marcy noticed all the work she'd done.

"Lisa honey I've never seen this house so pretty, you've done wonders with it." Lisa beamed under her praise feeling pride in her first home.

"It was always a mess when John lived here alone. I used to dread coming in here." Lisa felt hesitant but said,

"Thanks Mom, is it all right to call you mom?"

"It surely is, in fact I would be disappointed if you didn't feel like calling me mom." Lisa smiled and said "guess we best fix lunch now."

"You're right those hungry mouths will be home soon, and thanks Lisa for inviting me over."

They took their meals together in their own home. Lisa was a good cook. About once a week Marcy invited them to join them in their home usually on Sunday; it was enjoyable, fun for them all.

The next two months literally flew by. It was difficult for Lisa to move around being due in about a month. John was there for her whenever she needed him but he was working extra hard with the men on the farm. The horse vet was a regular on the scene as the mares time came nearer. Lisa wished she could work with the mares, she knew how they felt. Even Amos who wasn't sentimental on the surface was fussing over the mares. Yes, John was keeping himself busy. So far the only beer he'd had was on the back porch with his dad and Amos!

The day the letter arrived for Lisa was cold and wet. Except for a slight case of toxemia, and a little spotting of blood once, all seemed well. John brought in the mail that evening, and tossed it on the kitchen table. It was the usual, several ads, a couple of bills, and a pink envelope addressed to Lisa. No reason to suspect anything wrong. There was no return address but Lisa guessed it was from Sally and she simply forgot to add it. Dinner was nearly ready, so she simply moved all the mail to the counter to read later in the evening. She didn't even look at the handwriting! John had already gone to bed, and was dozing off when he heard a blood-curdling scream. He leaped out of bed and ran into the kitchen. Lisa's face was contorted in pain and she appeared to be way too red in the neck and face. She was waving a letter at him,

"How could you," she said!

"How could I what?" John replied worried sick. "Is it the baby?" he asked?

"No, it's not the baby but I would sure like an explanation from you about this letter, you—you Asss—!"

By now John had turned a sickly white, as Lisa handed him the letter, the one that came that day in the pink envelope. Tears coursed down her cheeks and she really didn't look well at all.

It began with: *"Dear Lisa,*
You don't know me but I know you. I feel so sorry for you being in your condition with that bastard child and all. What a shame it happened like that. It should have been John's child you are carrying instead of that devil's spawn of yours. I believe the newspaper said it was a Frank Windsor, is that correct?
At any rate I just wanted to wish you well, and let you know that John and I have been a real hot item for a long time. I see no reason for that to change just because he's married to you now.
Best Wishes Anonymous—
PS I thought you looked real pretty at your wedding—considering."

By the time John finished reading the letter his face turned from white to beat red with anguish, and anger. Lisa felt weak in the knees, feeling faint, and started to fall. John grabbed her picked her up and carried her to bed.

"Honey listen, this is all a big mistake, and it isn't what you think I promise. Just let me explain it to you. I never dreamed anyone could be this evil. I blame myself more though for not telling you about this witch before we were married. I owed you that, and I am so sorry my love."

Between Lisa's sobs she told him she wanted to die.

"I can't believe this" she said. John held onto her trying to soothe her to no avail. Finally she twisted away from him saying,

"Don't touch me!" Lisa turned toward the wall and didn't utter another word. It was horrifying for John. For the first time in his life he felt that he understood how a murder could happen. 'If I could get my hands on Stella, I'd kill her.'

CHAPTER 15

After a long and sleepless night, Lisa was in the same condition, or worse than the night before. John left her alone long enough to find his mother. He wanted to ask her to help, get her advice, and have her stay with Lisa while he went to work. After telling Marcy, she shook her head at him saying,

"Dear God John that was really stupid, not telling her yourself. If you had, it might have defused the effects of the letter at least to some degree."

"I know," he said "now the damage is done. Please stay with her while I help Amos and Dad. If she isn't better I'll take her to the doctor later today. Please, get word to me if anything changes, or you need me."

Marcy was shaken badly by this latest sad happening. She said,

"Of course John," she gave him a quick hug before hurrying over to their house to stay with her. After checking Lisa and trying to talk to her with no response, she kissed her dry cheek. Marcy's hands trembled as she tucked her in with another blanket. Lisa was shivering. She left the bedroom to phone Lisa's parents to tell them what had happened. She dreaded it, but they had to know as soon as possible. Oh how Marcy hated to tell them after all the bad things that all ready had happened. As she dialed the number she thought 'what a horrendous year this has been now this!'

"Hello Grace, it's Marcy. I'm afraid I've some unpleasant news. No Lisa isn't in labor, but something awful happened." After explaining the whole thing Grace said, "I'll be on my way up as soon as I tell Jeb, and pack a few things. I have to be there with her, maybe it'll help. Jeb can't get away with foaling going on but I can call him daily to keep him up on things. See you late tonight if it's all right?"

"Of course Grace we'll be expecting you, I'll have your room ready, see you then." As soon as John could he hurried home.

"Any change Mom?"

"No nothing, I think you should take her right now. Oh and Grace is on her way up, Jeb won't be coming.

"Small wonder," John said, "with foaling so near, we're in the midst of it too. Okay, I will get going and will phone you as soon as I know what the doctor says." Marcy stayed and helped John get Lisa into the car and covered her with a blanket it was getting colder. At the office, it didn't take Dr. Simon five minutes to see that Lisa needed to be hospitalized. She needed both medical monitoring, and psychiatric help. He told him she was in shock from reading the letter. John explained and told him all that had taken place since the letter arrived.

"Try not to worry though I know it's near impossible, we'll be in close touch with you. I'll have you go with her to the hospital to have her admitted, then see her to her room. I will also have her OB-GYN examine her, make sure the baby is all right as well as Lisa. "With any luck she could be home in a week." John grimaced, saying "That would be so great with Christmas nearly here. Tonight we were going to put our tree up. Thank you Doctor Simon, I'll be right back to take Lisa to the hospital, and have her admitted. I need a minute to phone home and tell the family what's happening." As he dialed the familiar number John felt waves of guilt and deep sadness contrasted with all the joy of their wedding and the happy weeks following.

That night after Grace arrived they were a subdued group tired and worried about both Lisa and the baby. Grace phoned Lisa's room and could hardly get her to say hello. All she said was "Hi." She listened as she told her she loved her, and then the nurse hung up the phone. By that time Grace was weeping, and Marcy went to her and hugged her. There were tears in both their eyes. They would visit her in the morning. There was little sleep for anyone on this night. Grace, hardly slept at all, just dozed on and off. Marcy was glad John had already gone home. The last thing he needed was to see how upset they were.

Something odd happens to the perpetrator of a cruel and sinful act. Stella was nervous the day after she mailed the poisonous letter to Lisa. By the following day she was having twinges of needling fear, and regret. John would know in less than a second who sent it! She began looking behind her when she left her apartment fearing what he might do. With just enough intelligence to realize what it would be like if the shoe were on the other foot, yet stupid enough not to know she'd caused him such grief he'd never look at her again. The reality was she didn't give a damn about Lisa, only that she'd lost what she wanted which of course was John. 'My mind is playing tricks on me,' she thought. Stella wasn't sleeping well at all. She was seen hanging around the entrance to Mason property by one of the workers. He knew who she was, and told John about it! As soon as he heard, he drove to the *Meade* police station and filed a restraining order against her. He wasn't taking any more chances. John wanted

Stella as far away as possible, off Mason land for good. The very day she was served with the order Stella packed and left Kentucky. She moved back to Florida where she came from as a teenager. By the time this news reached John, he was relieved, and with a deep sigh said, "At Last—Good Riddance!"

Being pregnant, Lisa couldn't have anything except *Tylenol* in the way of medication. With all the complications, coming home for Christmas just wasn't to be. It was a very quiet and rather sad holiday for everyone. Grace left within two days of arrival with the understanding she would keep in close touch. Remarkably she seemed not to blame John for this last sad turn of events. Grace was a remarkable woman wise with the years. She understood that John certainly had a social and private life before Lisa. The main problem with Lisa was the years of torture at the hands of Frank Windsor!

When Lisa went into labor, they phoned John as they transferred her from maternity into a delivery room at *Meade Community Hospital*. He was there within half an hour holding Lisa's hand. For the moment at least she seemed to be more responsive toward him holding onto his hand as tight as he held hers. Her water broke and startled them both. Before birth came, about an hour of hard labor was endured without complications. On December 30, 1984 at 7:58 PM Alexander Windsor Mason was born. A healthy baby boy of 8 pounds 4 ounces and 21 inches long arrived. When the doctor laid him on top of Lisa's stomach she reached down and touched his dark wet hair. "He's beautiful Lisa, John said, looks just like you." A very tired young woman gave him a weak smile.

Jeb took time off work to drive up with Grace to see their daughter, and first grand baby. The first grandchild for both families and they were very proud of this adorable little boy. Out of respect for the senior Windsor's and all the kindness shown over the years Lisa and John chose Windsor as his middle name. Like it or not, biologically he is a Windsor, they are grandparents too. Their health wasn't good, but they were very happy to hear about little Alex. In talking with her parents Lisa asked them to take a few photos to them.

"They were always very good to me when growing up!"

"Yes, they were Lisa, and to us too. It will be a joy to share him with them. We know you aren't up to it now, but hope all of you will visit us later on and then perhaps the Windsor's can see him."

Both Jeb and Grace had to go home before Lisa was discharged with Alex. They took several photos to share with both Sally, and the Windsor's.

Her doctors were waiting to assess how Lisa was feeling emotionally after the birth. Remarkably she seemed better and was discharged with a mild anti-depressant to help her over all the stress she'd been through.

When they arrived home with little Alex, there were flowers everywhere from Marcy and Bill. Marcy and one of their women employees cleaned their home. It was absolutely perfect when they arrived. There were also many baby gifts from the families and from friends. Marcy took care to be sure there was nothing unexpected, no unwanted gifts! There weren't any of course, but this last incident was about the last straw. Bill said, "Don't take any chances my love, those kids can't have anymore sadness. Perhaps now at last this will give them a fresh and happier start to their marriage." Marcy also thought it a good idea to offer to baby sit in a month or so. That way they could have a night out for supper and maybe a movie. She would mention it to them later.

John and Lisa were very considerate and courteous to each other but the light hearted teasing seemed gone for now. There was also something else, a distancing of emotions between them. John knew his behavior wasn't exemplary before they were married but he'd been very faithful and attentive during Lisa's pregnancy. He felt hurt and couldn't express it to anyone. It just built up within like a sore that was being picked at every day.

Lisa was a good mother, loving and tender with Alex. She would hold his little hands as she nursed him and kiss his forehead. Many times John would come in during the day and hear her sweet voice singing a lullaby to him. After supper John wanted time to hold him and loved cuddling him.

"Lisa, I didn't know babies smelled so sweet. He looks more like you every day, he has your same deep sparkling eyes and that smile, Wow!"

"I think he's cute, but he doesn't always smell that sweet, trust me!" John looked up at Lisa startled by her comment, hoping she felt better, happier. She was smiling at him and he was thrilled beyond words it brought a pang of longing deep within him. It was Lisa he longed for.

"Come here little mother," he said. Lisa left the table to stand in front of John and Alex.

"How are you feeling love, come on down here so I can kiss your cheek." She happily obliged, and sat on the arm of the over stuffed chair. They both cooed to Alex and played with him until it was time to nurse him, and put him to sleep for the night. All signs of hurt and bitterness seemed to have evaporated for the moment. Perhaps a combination of anti-depressant, the counseling and birth of Alex helped heal Lisa's mind.

That night when they climbed into bed together he held her for the first time in ages and kissed her good night. His kiss had a way of letting Lisa know some of the tenderness he felt for her and she returned his kiss but it lacked passion. John understood and thought to himself, she needs more time.

When her eight-week checkup with the doctor came, he released her. He said, "young lady you and your husband can safely resume your sexual relations whenever you're ready." Lisa made no comment except to say, "Thank you doctor."

It was the weekend at *Mason Haven* a quieter time. John was well aware it had been a little over eight weeks since Alex's birth though

Lisa said nothing. He had hopes of loving Lisa in a physical way expressing his love at last in this most intimate of ways. He came home early, helped her with the baby and cleaned up the kitchen after they ate. When she finished feeding him it was John who gave Alex his bath. All the while he thought of later that night in anticipation, how he would touch her gently and with loving tenderness. As soon as Alex was quiet John showered and slipped on his shorts and jeans. He went to Lisa and put his arms around her waist.

"Honey you're even prettier now than the first time I saw you. Having our baby has added a special glow. You're the most desirable woman I've ever seen. I have a surprise, come on Lis you'll love it." He led her into the bath. It was warm with bubbles and he'd lit candles. "Lisa love, let me give you your bath." There was a sound in his voice so soft that made Lisa say yes.

John slowly undressed her taking his time feasting his eyes as he took off the last of her clothes. His voice was raw with emotion, "Turn around love," he began massaging her neck and back right where his own body was sore. He ached for her to touch him—anywhere. After bathing her just as careful as he'd washed Alex he toweled her dry. "Sit down Lisa; let me brush your hair." This was something he'd never done before it was instinctive. She loved it. "No one has ever done this for me John thank you. Not since I was a little girl and my mom—." He silenced her with a soft kiss on the mouth teasing her lips with his. He blew out the candles and carried her to their bed. In the silence before they came together for the first time. John heard what he'd longed to hear for all these many weeks. "I love you John," she said and meant it with her whole heart. She kissed him with the only kiss she knew how to give. John would teach her new ways to kiss.

CHAPTER 16

It is early March 1985. Gramma Marcy and grampa Bill are going to baby-sit with Alex for the first time over night. His parents have a date for dinner and dancing to celebrate a belated valentine's day. It will be their first night out since Alex was born. Both homes are buzzing with preparation. Alex was fed and John took him up to the main house for the night along with a bundle over flowing with more baby paraphernalia than they could possibly use. Lisa is getting dressed to go and misses him already! They planned to pick him up after breakfast in the morning; that is if she could stand being separated from him that long. John wasn't much better with a whole list of instructions he proceeded to explain to his mom.

"Hey," she finally said smiling "John I managed to take care of you ya know, we'll be fine quit worrying! Go—and have a good time with Lisa."

"Okay Mom, I'm on my way." John grinned at her and made the run over to their house hollering as he went in, "Lisa honey, are you ready?" She was just zipping up the back of her new dress, catching a glimpse of her side view as she flipped the top of the zipper down. What she saw pleased her. She smiled at herself, her now slender body in a vivid blue sheath dress looked good. Lisa was stunning to look at. John rounded the corner of their bedroom and whistled at her.

"Thanks John," she said, "And yes I'm almost ready. Just help me fasten my necklace please. You're lookin very spiffy tonight yourself!"

He gave her a winning smile, "thanks," he said. John's eyes were the color of deep blue water. Tonight they were extra bright with pleasure. His rugged handsome face was usually tan but was lighter now. The sun hid behind heavy clouds. Spring was late in coming and June was usually cloudy as well.

They left for town in Lisa's Chevy. John was pleased, thinking how this car was the perfect gift for her. What he felt was akin to smug, thinking how things were going. The reservation was for 7:00 PM at the old historic *Blue Grass Hotel*. They enjoyed a delicious supper with wine, then relaxed and danced the night away till closing.

"We should have done this sooner," John said. They were both feeling relaxed and grateful for Marcy's idea to baby sit. Gramma thought they should make it a standing date each month! They'd kicked the idea back and forth and agreed to take her up on it.

All the way home Lisa thought mostly of Alex, they'd phoned the house twice! John on the other hand was thinking, 'can't this car move any faster, I want to make love to my wife!' I suppose you would consider this a gender paradox.

"Sweetheart, I am so proud to be your husband, showing you off tonight was—it's hard to put in words…Very special! I hope you had as much fun as I did?"

Lisa shifted her position in the seat so her head could lean on the backrest.

"Yes I had a wonderful time," she said watching his profile, 'hmmm' she thought a second. Smiling she said "I feel like some sort of princess the way we sat there being served in such a fancy place. A little like being *Cinderella* I suppose." John was elated.

"I'm so happy Lisa, I love you." He waited for her response.... A short pause lingered between them before she said,

"I love you too John. Being your wife is a dream come true for me. I wish I could have met you sooner, and under different circumstance." Her voice sounded wistful, she thought to herself, 'if only all wishes and dreams came true.'

"Let's not think about what might have been, no regrets okay Lis? Let's enjoy the rest of our night together."

"Of course you're right John, I'm sorry it's just, oh darn it. I can't help but wish that you'd been my boyfriend in school and that I'd never even lived at *Windsor Stock Farm*." They were turning into the drive home now.

"Lisa, it's time to let all of that go and live—now, please try to forget as best you can. Besides, even if that could have been, you'd have been so far behind me in school I'd of thought you were a teeny bopper!" They both laughed out loud at that idea because it was absolutely true. John graduated and was in college when Lisa was in Junior High.

"Oh well, a happy thought anyway," she said.

As they were getting undressed Lisa remembered something.

"Know what?"

"What?" John asked.

"Doctor Simon said much the same thing to me, day before yesterday, when I went for my appointment. He said it was time to forget, time to heal. I know that's true, but darn, it's hard. Sometimes I can't stop the memories and my head hurts with it." John drew her into his arms saying:

"Yes love it is time to heal, I promise to take your pain away" he kissed her with more passion than Lisa felt in return. They made love with tenderness and affection, then slept.

Later, around 4:00 in the morning Lisa woke them both screaming. She cried out in fright and trembled uncontrollably. She often had nightmares but this one was worse.

"Shhh, it's all right honey I'm right here you're okay. You're safe in our own home and nobody will ever hurt you again, I'll take care of you."

'Dear God' he thought 'why? This is so unfair.' Lisa's mind was in torment. In her dream Frank was still very much alive and he chased her endlessly. She was hysterical in spite of John's attempts to soothe her. He finally got them both up and had Lisa in the kitchen so she'd be fully awake. They sat in silence and sipped hot tea laced with honey till she could finally compose herself. It was nearly dawn. Not exactly the night they were hoping for, but it had moments of happiness. 'For now this will have to be enough' John thought.

As time passed, one reoccurring fearful thought resurfaced in Lisa's mind, 'I'm going insane. How will I be able to be a good mother or wife then?' In silence within her heart she prayed, 'dear God, help me please I don't understand why I can't be normal like everyone else. John is so precious and dear, I want to make love to him with the same passion that he feels for me—but I can't.' A tear ran and she never noticed it. Tears were a part of her every day life. 'If only,' just then Lisa noticed the time. It's 12:00 PM, 'I have to hurry' she thought. 'My appointment with Doctor Simon is at 1:00 P.M.' She finished bathing and dressing Alex. Now that he was older he was easier to care for. His small arms and legs went into his clothes easier. 'It seemed to me that when you were first born, you were a little like trying to dress a limp noodle.' This thought brought a smile, a bright happy thought! Alex had Lisa's open face look, the kind of look that all babies have. Below his near black curly hair he always had a look of surprise, and wide-eyed innocence. Even when he pouted and his mouth puckered up the look had appeal. His little nose turned up slightly. The bridge of that nose was where both she and John liked to kiss him.

"Hey little man" she cooed "you are so handsome and momma's proud of you. You're going to visit gramma Marcy for awhile."

"Cookie" Alex said!

"Yes, I'm sure gramma will give you a cookie especially after I tell her how you ate such a good lunch."

Alex was twenty eight months old now and forming sentences.

"Before long you'll be wearing big men's pants like daddy, and go potty all by yourself." Marcy and Bill were both ready to help out in that department. Potty training would help them all. There was a potty-chair at both homes already.

"What a grownup boy you are Alex, step up now. Mom, we're here," she said.

"Come on in Lisa and Alex, I'm coming. Go ahead Lisa and I'll see you when you get home. Drive careful love!" Marcy and Lisa had an easy relationship with each other. Without knowing it Marcy give strength to Lisa by being supportive. She had a way of making everything seem all right in spite of the circumstance. She leaned over to Lisa kissing her goodbye on the cheek. Alex stood between them looking up at both their faces smiling.

"Cookie please," he plainly said.

"In a minute," gramma answered!

The receptionist met Lisa as she went in.

"Have a seat Mrs. Mason, Doctor Simon will be with you in a moment." She said thanks quietly, and sat starring out the window keeping to her own thoughts. Within minutes the doctor came out and invited her in.

"Lisa, how are you feeling today?"

"Fair" she answered. "When will this be over, will it ever be over? I'm so very tired I want to be well and lead a normal life. I don't like anxiety, nor feeling,—abnormal!"

"That is why we're doing all of this Lisa, all these treatments and your talking about your fears. All of it helps lead you a step further toward a normal life. Today I am going to try something new with your permission. I want to try Sodium Pentothal [thiopental] to relax you and help you purge all the deep-seated fears from your past. There is nothing for you to worry about I will be right here with you and it is similar to hypnosis. Okay?"

"Yes, I'll try anything that might help."

Doctor Simon called the nurse in to administer the sedative into her arm and then he gently began urging her back in time.

"You are at *Windsor Farm* Lisa," she began to sweat and tears came wetting her cheeks.

"It's all right I am with you" he assured her "nobody will hurt you. Where are you?"

Lisa whimpered saying, "Riding my horse after feeding it's a beautiful day. I'm on a trail that leads to the hills at the back, but I hear something." Fear was etched clearly on her face as she relived what?

"Take it easy Lisa, just tell me what happens."

"I hear a horse coming, behind me. I'm scared!"

"Why?" he asked.

"It might be Frank chasing me again." Lisa's respiration was heavy, her heart raced.

"Calm down and just tell me what happens next. Has Frank followed you on horseback before?"

"Yes, lots of times it's my fault, I tried to get Sally to ride with me but she couldn't. I should never have gone alone."

"Lisa, are you listening to me?"

"Yes" she said. "No matter what happened, it was never your fault you were not to blame for any of it. You were only a child and he was an adult much stronger than you were. Now what is happening?"

Lisa squirmed on the couch as she struggled with her inner demons.

"I kick my horse to go faster, and can hear the other horse running too. I turn and see him, it's Frank and he is laughing at me. I can hear him and he said:"

"Might as well rein that horse in, I'm gonna get cha anyway."

"Lisa" Dr. Simon said, "lay quiet for a minute and listen to me, Frank can't hurt you he's dead. Listen to me, he's dead. This is just a bad memory that will leave you now." Doctor Simon made a notation on Lisa's chart. She was pursued many times on horseback by Frank. 'No wonder she didn't want to ride anymore! She's been suppressing this memory and associates riding with rape.'

"Tell me what happened next."

"Frank ran his horse along side of me and grabbed my reins and stopped me. He pulled me off the horse and threw me on the ground. It had been raining and it was cold and wet."

"Go on, what else."

"He pushed me over on my stomach, he pulled my pants down and he-he."

"Lisa, remember he can't hurt you now, okay what else?"

"He put his penis in my bottom and it hurt so bad. The more I cried the more he pushed and hurt me worse."

"Alright Lisa, that's enough now. Rest, sleep and when you wake up you will feel a lot better. Did you hear me?"

"Yes, I hear you Doctor Simon." Lisa slept for the rest of her session as the doctor completed his notes on her chart. 'Doctors never get emotionally involved' he reminded himself. This case tore at the fiber of his heart and he had a hard time remaining impersonal with this young woman.

CHAPTER 17

Over the next two years, Lisa was in and out of treatment in the psychiatric ward of the local hospital. Dr. Simon tried her on stronger anti depressants. Nothing seemed to quell her symptoms of depression, or her growing paranoia. Her headaches continued, along with bouts of uncontrollable weeping. John and Lisa were tired; her dreams left them exhausted, and disrupted their sleep. When her screams awakened Alex it was heart wrenching. It took time and energy that neither had to reassure him. It was becoming more difficult for everyone to cope with daily life. The sad fact was Lisa wasn't improving as they'd hoped. She was conscientious in her attempts; she followed all her doctor's advice to no avail. In an ironic way even that worked against her; having a negative effect on her already low moral, and self-esteem.

In the hope change would help, John took Lisa and Alex to spend time with her parents and Sally in Georgia. They went at least twice a year to visit and also spent some holidays together. Lisa and Sally remained good friends but she wasn't able to give Lisa anything except moral support. That, she gave to her generously. Jeb and Grace were always there for her, John, and his parents too. They all spent many hours talking and offering support. They listened with a sympathetic ear, and showered her with all the love they had.

With time, John grew more and more discouraged. He continued loving her faithfully, no doubts. He also did all he could to help with Alex.

Lisa would sometimes bring him with her to the paddocks and barns. She still smiled when she saw Warrior in the pasture and enjoyed being with the horses. She also helped some with the halter training of the foals while Alex was napping. Marcy gladly stayed with him so she could work the foals. As soon as Tag saw her he'd leave John and run to greet her, and oh how Tag loved Alex! He displayed his love as all dogs do with much tail wagging and wiggling in general all over. They'd both smile at this, it seemed Alex had inherited both John and Lisa's love for animals. John wondered why she wouldn't ride anymore; he hadn't spoken with Doctor Simon since her last appointment. Her parents said she used to love to go riding. Now he couldn't get her on a horse, not even when they bought a pony for Alex on his birthday. They hoped Lisa would ride with John and Alex for fun, and recreation, but she still refused without reason. Then John met with Dr. Simon for his update on Lisa's progress, and he understood. They hoped this could be over come for all their sakes. This latest finding made John furious. He felt like pounding on something solid. He cut and split a lot of firewood for all their homes.

He remained devoted, but little by little began drifting back to the local bars. There is never a shortage of bars in any town and *Meade* was no exception. Sometimes he'd go with Amos, more often he'd go alone and just spend the evening talking horses and watching sporting events on the large screen TV with the locals. John wasn't drinking heavy but still drank too often, which was too much. His parents and Amos knew, and wished he'd go light on the liquor they were concerned for his, and his family's future.

Oddly Lisa seemed oblivious to his drinking though on some level she must have known. After all they slept in the same bed even though their lovemaking had dwindled down till it was nearly non existent. She couldn't respond, and John was keenly aware and felt her passive way of allowing him to love her was wrong. It made him feel monstrous, as if he, like Frank were taking advantage of her. This was without doubt the fuel, which drove him to drink more! John felt confused by what the doctor was telling him when he went for monthly meetings to hear how she was doing. He often thought, 'I hate all of this that she is going through and what it's doing to our marriage.'

It was obvious to Dr. Simon that Lisa was in crisis and was having a nervous break down. She endured shock treatments as a last resort during one stay, and that seemed to help for a while. She was calmer, less full of anxiety. The medication they gave her was both a blessing and a curse. It helped even her mood swings, but left her mind foggy.

'My heart aches for her,' John knew what heart ache felt like. 'She doesn't have any of this pain and misery coming.' Her doctor told him he would use further hypnoses with Lisa and possibly Sodium Pentothal again. A means to learn what, or if she was suppressing any other bad memories. John was willing to allow whatever might help as long as Lisa agreed to the treatment. To release her of all the hurt would be an answer to all their prayers.

On coming home one morning after being in *Meade,* the house was in total silence. He had been drinking heavier than usual and stumbled into their bedroom close to dawn. There was just enough light to see the outline of Lisa's body in the moonlight. She was lying on her side with her long hair tumbled loose on her pillow. The window was open. It was a warm night and honeysuckle permeated the air. He stripped off, and climbed into bed next to her. With his finger he traced the outline of her beautiful face so lightly she hardly felt it yet she stirred, and turned over exposing her naked breasts and the curve of her slim hips.

The next thing he knew he'd made love to her, and again he felt pangs of guilt. Lisa put her hand on his saying, "it's okay John really. I'll just wash up and be right back." They both went to sleep then until Alex woke them at around seven o'clock. Neither gave it anymore thought. They went on with their days work, Lisa at home with her chores, and with Alex. John was late, going off to work with Amos and his dad. Lisa looked out after breakfast, and watched him go, loving him as he ambled off with Tag at his heels to the barn.

Within about six weeks from the night John made love to Lisa she suspected she could be pregnant-again! It hadn't been confirmed, but she was late and was already feeling queasy as she cooked breakfast. The memory of nausea in the morning stirred thoughts of back home. It stood out like a neon sign in her memory.

"Oh No," she said aloud! 'I can't help it, I don't want to be pregnant, not now'. The idea over whelmed her.

'How am I going to get through this she wondered if it's true. I won't tell anybody unless I am. But what else could it be', she wondered. 'It isn't the flu!' Lisa hurried getting Alex ready so she could take him to Marcy for an hour or so.

"Momma, where are we going?"

"Not now Alex" she said as she dialed the number; Marcy picked it up on the first ring.

"Hi Mom, could you baby sit in about ten minutes for an hour or so?"

"Sure bring the little man over I'll be glad to" she said. Lisa dropped him off explaining to him that she had an errand to run. She drove to church to be alone, to think and to pray!

'It's so peaceful here, why won't my mind rest instead of spinning so fast. This is where we were married,' she reasoned 'and it's a beautiful church. Help me God. Take this bitterness from me if you can she pleaded. Please, don't let me be pregnant not now, not yet! You know I want John's child but it's too soon.'

Light streamed in through the stained glass windows shinning on Lisa's head. There was no one to appreciate her devotion, and prayer except the most important, the presence of God's Spirit.

'Give me strength' she prayed over and over. Lisa stayed in the cool comfort of the sanctuary until she felt stronger and more peaceful. She put her rosary away, and drove home.

"Hi Mom, was Alex a good boy?"

"He's always good for his gramma" Marcy said, "I love the time we spend together."

"More cookies please," he said to them both! His speech was improving daily. Alex was very bright.

"Let's go home now Alex, momma has a few things to do, and you can help!"

"Help" he repeated with a big sweet smile. She thanked Marcy with a hug and drove home.

"We're going to cook and you can stir." He toddled over to a kitchen chair and began to push it toward Lisa.

"What are you doing Alex?"

"Helping you! I'm getting ready to stir!"

"Okay, but just sit in the chair till it's time please and I'll give you something to hold."

"What?"

"A spoon of course."

"Oh, what kind of spoon?"

"Well, Alex it's a very large one and I'll give you a bowl too so you can practice stirring here at the table while I get things ready."

Lisa was bending down getting the bowl as Alex made good use of the table with the wooden spoon she'd given him.

"You needn't bang it so hard love, here's the bowl and some water to stir."

"Thank you," he said. Lisa began chopping the ingredients to make chili for supper.

"We're having cornbread with chili and salad tonight."

"What does it taste like?"

'Questions, endless questions' Lisa thought smiling at him. 'I don't mind' she patiently thought, 'he is such a love.'

"It tastes very good, you'll have to wait and see."

"Will I like it?" Alex was persistent. It was plain to see that he was interested in everything around him. He adored his momma!

"I think so, at least the corn bread, and I'm fixing apple sauce and special chili."

"What kind a special?" He asked. "My you ask a lot of questions young man. It's chili without a lot of spice, just right for a boy your age!"

"What's spice?"

"Seasonings Alex, the cornbread is ready for you to stir." Lisa put the heavy bowl on the table with all the cornbread ingredients.

"Here, honey let me help you stir."

"NO, me do it myself—please."

"All right sonny just try to keep it inside the bowl."

"I will, I do it good." Lisa began chopping the onions, and stripping the green chilies that John loved when the knife slipped. "Dang it," she said.

"Momma, what's wrong?"

"Nothing really love except your momma has a small cut on her finger. Come with me to get a bandage Alex and then we'll finish supper."

"You're a sweet boy, and I love you."

By the time supper was simmering Alex was ready for a nap. She put him down, and dialed her GYN doctor to make an appointment.

"Hello, yes I can hold." The quiet of waiting caused Lisa to drum her fingers on the table. 'Why is it I have to wait and wait just to make an appointment' she wondered. 'Oh well, I suppose'—

"Yes, this is Lisa Mason, I want an appointment with the doctor for as soon as possible." There was a pause as the receptionist brought up Lisa's records on the computer screen.

"Would you prefer AM or PM?"

"I'd rather have afternoon please."

"Alright how about next week July 16th at 2:00 o'clock."

"That's fine thank you, and I'll see you then, goodbye."

'Making the appointment' Lisa thought 'will ease my mind.' Instead it made her more anxious wanting to know what the exam would show. She stirred the chili, and then dropped into the rocking chair and stared off into space.

John came through the door saying,

"Hi sweetheart how's' my love feeling, you're looking extra pretty today."

"Quiet John, you'll wake Alex."

"Sorry Lis, I thought he'd be up by now. Do you mind if I wake him after I wash up?"

"No honey, actually he should be up by now, time got away from me. Supper is almost ready I just need to toss the salad."

After the kitchen table was cleared, and dishes done John went in to shower. Lisa dialed Marcy.

"Hi Mom, I have another favor to ask." Marcy laughed good-naturedly, "ask away, will I get to watch Alex again for you?"

"As a matter of fact yes, I made an appointment for next week, a check up with the doctor. July 16th at 2:00 o'clock okay?"

"Yes, of course Lisa, are you feeling all right?"

"Pretty good, I just want to be sure, I've had a couple of slight dizzy spells, nothing serious, I'm just being careful."

"Good, does John know?"

"Not yet, but I'm going to tell him tonight, just hope he won't be too worried. You know how he is about my health!"

"Yes, I do and for good reason young lady, we all love you very much."

"I know you do and I love you too. Thanks mom, you and dad have a good night."

"We will, and you too. Goodnight and sweet dreams!"

CHAPTER 18

July sixteenth dawned hot and humid, it rained during the night. When it's eighty plus degrees on a Kentucky summer day it's sweltering! No one seems to mention it though, least of all the Mason's. They were all born here and used to the humidity. Lisa never noticed it because Georgia was just as hot and humid, perhaps more so.

After John left for work, Lisa took Alex out to pull weeds in their small gardens on the east and south sides of the house. Back in May she asked for help with the spading. She arranged two beds one for vegetables and the other in front for all sorts of flowers. She let Alex help her pull weeds first in the vegetable patch now in front. Lisa was admiring the variety of colorful flowers.

"Oh, no Alex honey that's not a weed, here let me show you. This one is a weed with the flat leaves, let the colored ones stay. Then we'll pick a bouquet when we're finished weeding."

"Boofee," he said.

Lisa pronounced it for him, "say bow—kay."

"What's a 'boow-kkey' momma?"

"They're flowers that we can pick to take to gramma Marcy honey. You can help me we'll do it together."

"Oh good, can we pick them all, is it time now?"

"No not all of them, that would be too many flowers. We're not quite finished but very soon. We'll put gramma's flowers in water so they'll stay fresh."

"Momma, what's fresh?" Lisa smiled at him; "well young man fresh is—. I'll show you in a little bit no more questions for now please!" Lisa nearly began explaining how flowers droop without water but then thought 'no I'm not getting the questions started again. I'll never finish in time. Gee whiz,' she thought smiling to herself. 'What a boy!'

They picked the bouquet for Marcy and put them in a small bucket of water in the shade.

Later, on his way out the door after lunch John hollered a reminder,

"Honey, don't forget to come find me, and tell me what the doctor said." Lisa didn't tell John what she suspected, just that she was going for a checkup.

"I sure will, before I pick up Alex, bye John." He gave her a kiss and left. The thought of telling him—if she was pregnant caused her to sigh. Alex was all ready for his nap at gramma's. They bathed together and were on their way to the main house with the flowers.

"Just a minute honey, momma will open the door for you."

"Wanta hold the flowers for gramma," he said.

"Here, Alex, and you can give them to her too." Marcy saw them coming and opened the front door. "Hello Alex, hi Lisa—oh my are those pretty flowers for me?"

"Yes Gramma here," he said smiling pushing them into her hands.

"Thank you both very much." Marcy hugged them both, then said goodbye to Lisa.

"See you in a while, Alex and I will have a nap together."

"Thanks Mom, talk to you when I get back. I'm going to let John know first, then I'll come here."

"Okay honey, don't worry, I'll see you then."

Lisa drove straight to the doctor's office in down town *Meade* arriving a little early. After signing in she had a short wait before the nurse escorted her into an examining room.

"Hello Mrs. Mason" and then took Lisa's vitals making the notations on her chart.

"Any special reason you're here today other than a routine checkup?" Lisa frowned and said, "I suspect I might be pregnant."

"Oh" said the nurse. "When was your last period?"

Lisa knew exactly when.

"It was eight weeks and three days ago."

"Well, unless something else is going on, you very well could be. The doctor will be right in." She picked up a *Country Woman* magazine and began idly flipping through it not really seeing anything.

"Hello Lisa" the doctor said as he entered the room.

"I haven't seen you since your eight week checkup after Alex's birth. How's your family, John and Alex?"

"They're both fine thank you, Alex is three and into everything. He's very smart, and a good boy. John is doing great working hard on the farm, we all keep busy."

The doctor asked, "What can I do for you today, are you feeling well?"

"As a matter of fact I'm nervous, I think I may be pregnant. I wanted to wait until my sessions with Dr. Simon were over before having another baby."

"How are the sessions going?"

"Fair, but it's taking longer than any of us thought it would and I'm anxious for it to be over. The medication helps, but it's taking so long."

"I am truly sorry your counseling is taking longer than you thought. Now, let's get the suspense over and give you an exam then we'll have the answer. Put this on backward, the nurse and I will be back shortly."

"How long ago did you say your last period was?"

"A little over eight weeks ago."

"There is no doubt, you are pregnant Lisa, but I would think you're further along than two months, more like three. Are you sure about the time?"

"Yes Doctor, I'm very sure."

"I'd like you to make an appointment for a month from now. We'll do an ultrasound. However if you have any problems before, call the office and we'll work you in immediately. Congratulations to you both, my best wishes to your whole family. We'll take good care of you and your baby, all will be fine, you'll see!"

All the way home Lisa was preoccupied with what she just learned. 'Dear God' she thought, 'I am pregnant after all. Of course, with the way I've been feeling in the mornings, why should I be surprised. My legs are already feeling puffy, and I constantly need to pee. No—no—no, this isn't happening, it's all a bad dream. Please damn it, not yet Lord. All right, calm down you're almost home.' Unwanted tears burned her eyes and ran. 'I'm such a wimp damn it, I can't even control my emotions.' She let herself scream alone in the car. Lisa screamed so loud that her throat hurt. She parked the car near the barn. Before getting out she took out a whole wad of tissues and dried her face. 'I'll just sit here a moment and calm myself before

I see John.' Not three minutes passed before she heard him calling her.

"Lisa honey" as he came running. He opened the car door took one look and knew something was wrong.

"Spill it" he said. Lisa started sobbing and in-between she managed to say, "I'm pregnant John!"

"Get out sweetheart," he helped her out and took her in his arms. "I'm so sorry it's all my fault Lisa. I wanted another child but not until you were ready for it. Please forgive me Lis." She felt worse not wanting him to feel guilty. Their emotions built up against each other. It made them both feel worse. The bane of existence, guilt upon guilt!

"John, please don't feel bad, after all I'm your wife, I love you." John shifted his feet nervously and wrapped her tighter in his arms.

"Let me hold you a little longer, just for a minute or so more love. I need that, we both do. We'll get through this somehow, Lisa I adore you. Tell you what, get in and wait in the car a minute. I'll go tell Amos and Dad that I'm quitting early today. We'll talk more, then go pick up Alex together and go out for supper tonight."

"Alright John, go ahead that sounds good," she said.

The next week Lisa and John were back walking after supper with Tag and Alex. Tag led the way with Alex close behind running as fast as his chubby legs could go. Evenings were warm to hot depending on which day in August. They were waiting for the next appointment with lots of anticipation. August 20th would tell them what was happening inside Lisa's growing belly. Walking seemed to help keep the swelling at bay. She elevated her legs at night, and between chores. Alex is such a love, but a real hand full to chase after. His laughter and Tag's barking was a pleasant sound to their ears. It was as if the dog knew Alex was just a little guy and was extra gentle with him.

"Come back Tag," John yelled at him, "they're getting too far ahead." Lisa smiled at John as the two came bounding back toward them.

"What did you think of your folks reaction to our news?"

"They have a right to their opinion Lisa, and I think I tend to agree with them. After all, you were just sleeping that night and I'm the one who started the love making."

"Now wait a minute," she said. "If I was asleep, and looking pretty like you said, then maybe it was my fault!" Lisa received a slight smile from John for her effort.

"Yes honey, but you aren't in anyway ready for another child."

"Well" she said, "at least my morning sickness is gone, no more nausea. I appreciate your having breakfast with your folks the last weeks so I didn't have to smell bacon cooking. That smell really gets to me for some reason."

"Come on Alex, come Tag, let's head for home now, momma has had enough walking for tonight!"

"I'm not surprised that my parents had the opposite reaction from yours. Mine were so pleased that I was expecting your baby. I think it's because they love you so much."

"That means a lot to me Lisa, and really my folks just feel protective of you with their reaction. By living close to us they know that you're not ready to have another baby."

"Oh, did I tell you what Dr. Simon said at our last meeting about your progress?"

"Nope you didn't," Lisa said.

"He was pleased, and said you seemed to have accepted the pregnancy very well under the circumstance. I know it's harder on you though, to go for appointments every week since he had to take you off all anti-depressant medication."

"Thanks to your mom for watching Alex for us while I keep my appointments. And as far as the medication, it's worth it to have a healthy baby. Other wise I'd have no peace of mind for worry over him or her!" Lisa was very brave through out the early stage of her pregnancy, and continued doing her best.

"Yes, of course you're right" John said, "I feel the same. And you know mom loves having his company, so does dad when he's around and not working with me, Amos and the other men."

August 20th came around in a hurry. It was 10:00 AM and the exam had just started. All of the Mason clan went to the appointment including Bill! He watched Alex, as Marcy came in and out of the examining room. She was in with Lisa, and John, when suddenly She came running out to Bill. "Holy Smoke" she clearly said. Alex immediately repeated it over and over while she talked.

"There are two babies, Bill, we're having twins! I'm going back in to see if I can learn what gender they are."

"Calm down Marcy" Bill told her.

"Alex, come back here to grampa."

"Coming soon" he said with a giggle.

"Come now please" grampa, said!

"Holy smoke, all right Grampa I love you."

Just then Marcy came out again sucking air in and looked rather pale.

"What's up Marcy," Bill asked? She spoke just above a whisper.

"It seems we are having fraternal twins a boy—and a girl. At least that's their best guess! They hope she can carry them through this coming February. No wonder she was growing much larger this time. Lisa is upset, and they're all trying to calm her down. I don't think any of them can believe it yet. I'm going to phone Lisa's parents, while you stay with Alex."

"Okay honey, but please settle down, do you want a cup of coffee?"

"Yes, but wait till I come back from the phone and we'll go together I could really use another cup."

"Hello Grace it's Marcy,—brace yourself. I know you were expecting this call, but you're not expecting this news. It's twins! They are ninety percent sure it's a boy and a girl, if it's true then they're fraternal!"

"Oh my, oh my" Grace said.

"Jeb come in here, Lisa is having twins, they think a boy, and a girl!" Jeb let out a shout that sounded something like "Whoops!"

"Okay you two, I gotta run now but we'll talk again tonight."

"Lisa? Oh well, she's upset but who wouldn't be with that news. Talk to ya later, Bye."

That evening Lisa was on the couch resting with her feet up. John was getting Alex ready for bed. The inside of Lisa's head was a mass of confusion and panic. 'I understand that I am having twins' she thought, 'but the idea of having twins—and Alex. That's a total of three kids, so soon it makes me crazy. Crazy that's me' as she stifled her feeling of hysteria. Lisa could hardly contain her desire to scream. 'I just got Alex potty trained with Marcy's help, now this. One baby would have been too many, and it's too damn soon' she thought! 'Hmm, let's see, and all I can take to relieve my symptoms is one *Tylenol*, that's crap! Sometimes I just wish I could disappear from the face of the earth, damn I hate this!' She had a lump in her throat she couldn't swallow just as John walked in.

"Honey, what can I do to help you?"

"Not a damn thing John," she said dripping with sarcasm. "Unfortunately you've already done it!"

John felt like he'd been slapped in the face. He was used to Lisa's mood swings but this seemed unfair and ridiculous.

"Thanks Lisa," he replied "I just wanted to tell you that the bed's turned down for you and Alex is asleep. I'm going out!"

"Fine I don't give a damn" she said, "And please, let that door hit your ass on the way out." Lisa went to bed angry, and without a twinge of guilt. That's how she felt at that moment. 'Wish I could drink a whole bottle of whiskey' she thought, and never looked in on Alex. She flopped face down, and stayed there till her belly hurt so bad she screamed with her hand over her mouth, to keep from waking him. 'I can smell my own body, maybe when he gets home he'll like the way I smell!' Lisa turned toward the wall and cried herself to sleep.

By the time John pulled into the parking lot and got out of the truck he was furious and felt like licking his wounds. 'She sure was being a bitch tonight pregnant or not' he thought! When he went into the *Water Trough* he saw someone he hadn't seen in years. It was Clarese Lampson, a woman who used to work as an extra hand at Mason's. She was a rough looking woman, but friendly with the guys and easy to talk to. She was sexy in a rough way. The guys flocked around her now. He bought a boiler maker downed it and joined them.

"Hey Clarese, how ya been" he called to her.

"Hello good lookin, how've you been John? Haven't seen you in a few years, you're a sight. How about a game of pool?"

"Sounds great," he said and they picked their cues and began playing. The rest of the guys just cleared away figuring John was interested in making a night of it. That he did, not going home till dawn and went straight to work wearing his dark glasses. He didn't return home until late that afternoon.

CHAPTER 19

After thinking about Alex and Lisa pretty well all day, he left work early and returned home to the sound of Alex crying. He was outside in the yard alone walking in circles repeating over and over, "Momma's sick—Daddy, Momma sick!"

"I know little man, and we'll take care of her, it'll be all right." John picked him up and went inside. He walked to the doorway and looked in. Lisa was staring at the ceiling and looked as if she was in a comma.

"Lisa," he called. She didn't answer him. John dialed his mom's number.

"Mom, have you talked to Lisa today?"

"I haven't, John is everything alright?"

"No it isn't" he said. "She's just lying on the bed and won't answer. Can I bring Alex over? He was outside alone crying and I doubt if he's had anything to eat today."

"Yes of course, bring him right now to stay the night." Soon as they were inside she hugged him, washed his hands and sat him down to supper. Marcy didn't mince words with John motioning him out the door so Alex couldn't hear. "Son you know I love you, but you were out all night. Amos and your dad said they saw you come in this morning. Bet you had a rough night and I think it's going to get rougher around here. With your permission I'm going to enroll Alex in pre-school tomorrow. He's the right age, and it's obvious Lisa isn't up to caring for him right now. You'd better go home, and call Doctor Simon. Tell him how she is, and see what he advises you do. Stay home tonight son!"

"I will Mom. I shouldn't have gone out last night and know it, I totally blew it." John ran home, and called the doctor. They spoke briefly, and made an early morning appointment. Then John hurried in to take care of Lisa. She was like a different person, totally withdrawn. John led her into the bath like a child and bathed her. Then into the kitchen to eat some soup. He ended up feeding her a few spoonfuls and that was all she'd swallow, except for a few sips of milk. She got up from the table and started out the front door.

"No Lisa."

All she said was "Alex?"

"He's all right honey, he's with mom for the night, she's feeding him. Come on sit down, and watch TV for a while." Lisa sat down and stared at the set without seeing. At about ten o'clock John changed the sheets and led her back to bed, she slept the night. John stayed on the couch.

Tired as he was he slept little wondering how this could possibly work out right. 'I've seen her and listened to her at her worse but this is totally different. Last night she was hostile, down right mean. A personality change different from what I've ever seen before, now this total withdrawal.'

'Shit' he thought, 'she's got to eat and I have to work. I can't put it all on mom. Maybe her folks? Nah, but I do need to phone them tomorrow and tell them how she is, and what the doctor says.' All of this ran through his mind. When he phoned Grace and Jeb they were understandably upset, and asked that he keep in close touch.

There are times when morning dawns to the bleakest of days. This was one of those days for John. The appointment was for 9:00 o'clock. She refused to eat breakfast twisting her head back and forth, and saying "No!" John helped her get dressed to go then she sat passive and docile while he phoned his mom to see how Alex was.

"He's fine son, he starts pre-school tomorrow half a day five days a week. It'll be good for him, get him ready for kindergarten. How's Lisa?"

"Not good, I'm about to leave with her, the appointment is at 9:00. Tell Dad I'll be to work soon after that, I'll stop in and see you and Alex first, and fill you in." Marcy felt depressed herself for all of them. When she had concern over their marriage she never guessed it would be this difficult. 'Poor John and Lisa' she thought, 'and Bill and I aren't too thrilled either!'

"Okay John, and good luck...."

"Thanks Mom we'll need it, the doctor said to pack some clothes for her and bring personal items. I suspect he's planning to keep her for awhile."

After examining Lisa Dr. Simon said, "I think it best to keep her for observation. I'll contact her GYN doctor and have him check her. I'll be in touch by phone with you in two days unless there is some change you need to know. Try not to worry!"

"All right Dr. Simon, I'll be home between 5:00 and 6:00 PM each day or you can always reach me through my parents. I believe you have their number."

"Yes I do, thanks John we'll take good care of Lisa and her babies. I learned in a conference call that she's having twins."

John drove home slowly, with all this weight on his mind. 'Worst of all' he thought 'was having to sign Lisa into the hospital without her permission. I feel guilty about that, but there was no other choice.' He drove past the church about a block, and stopped. On impulse he turned around and drove back parking the car. He hadn't done this in years not since he was confirmed as a kid. Without thinking he simply got out of the car and checked the door. It was open, he went in. It felt good and cool the sun streamed in through the stained glass windows. Each one with a station of the cross of Christ, he remembered being taught about that. There were a few old people up front praying. John walked down a few rows, bowed toward the altar and then knelt in prayer. He prayed for Lisa, Alex and for the babies she carried. 'They're mine too' was the thought that repeatedly ran through his mind. 'Please God keep them safe, especially Lisa.' He sat there praying, and thinking for half an hour or so, and felt better. 'Well John' he thought, 'time to go home to work.'

In that short drive he pondered 'why is it that man waits until he feels shattered before asking for God's help.' Darned if he could figure it out. He knew from teachings as a kid that spiritually God is here for us. 'Hmm just the way we humans are I guess.' He told his mom what the doctor said about Lisa. They were out in the yard. He hugged, and spoke with Alex, who had been happily occupied playing with both Tag and Cookie. Then he hurried off to work! Thank goodness kids are resilient...Not immune, but resilient!

From her physical appearance you'd think Lisa had nothing on her mind. The staff paid little notice of her unless they had a job they were to do for her such as checking her vitals. For most of them their job was rote, easier that way to distance themselves emotionally.

"Give me your arm Mrs. Mason so I can take your blood pressure," or "I need to draw blood," followed with "Thank you." The only exception was her daily session with Doctor Simon. He was extremely kind and cared deeply always doing his best to help. She either sat in her room staring out in the hall, or looked out the window. She rarely joined the other patients in the main living room where the TV blared. Lisa preferred her room to the din of noise and crude sounds that some of the patients made. Many of them were heavily sedated, others not sedated enough. They sometimes argued among themselves, and others simply rambled repetitive unintelligible words.

'Why' she wondered 'is it like this, I shouldn't be here. There is nothing wrong with me except I'm pregnant—with twins!' This thought repeated over and over in her mind, 'twins twins twins!' She guessed the repetitive thought was for the sole purpose that she would eventually accept the fact it was true. 'What I want to be false is true. Now there is a logical thought, see Lisa there's nothing wrong with you. It's them, all of them they are the unhinged ones.' Lisa watched the staff's routine, every detail. She decided she'd get out of here and go somewhere when the opportunity presented itself. 'I'm not sure where yet, but away.' She covered her mouth to keep from laughing. 'I wouldn't want them to hear me.

'What a shame' she thought, 'that I don't believe in abortion. If I did I would be free of this growing of what within? Parasites' she decided, 'yes, they are just like parasites. Oh well, only about four or five months to go.' This time she put both hands over her mouth to stop herself from screaming. 'Can't call attention to myself now can I' she kept hysteria just below the back of her throat. As a nurse walked by her room and looked in she questioned her.

"Mrs. Mason is your throat sore?"

"No ma'am," she said sarcastically. The nurse shrugged her shoulders and walked on past. Lisa was facing the hall so she could watch the comings and goings of the ward. She soon learned that the charge nurse pushed a buzzer to allow people in and out of the main double doors. 'I'm not a prisoner, but I feel like one.' The doctor explained that soon she'd have visitors and could go home on weekends. The doors were kept closed to protect her. 'Ha,' she thought!

To find out the exact location of the button she went to the desk and said, "I have a headache, may I have a *Tylenol* please?" While the nurse on duty checked her chart Lisa stood on her toes to see if she could find the location of the button. 'Yes, I see it, and all I need do is reach up and over the counter when no one's around.'

"Yes, Mrs. Mason you can have *Tylenol* the medication nurse will be around in about five minutes." Lisa thanked her saying she'd be in her room.

When the medication nurse dispensed her *Tylenol* she also gave her a warning. "If you can't eat more at meal times, your obstetrician has given an order to feed you fluids through an intravenous tube." Lisa ate more food that night. She lay awake late plotting her escape. When she was satisfied with her plan she tried to fall asleep. The first week patients weren't allowed visitors. 'This is my fifth day, and I don't want to see John, or anybody so I want out before then.'

The next morning was a warm September day. Lisa sipped her decaffeinated coffee nervously 'At least I won't need to worry about being cold' she thought, 'not even at night.' She carefully calculated her day and decided noon was her best chance to pull off the escape. Her small roll of belongings she'd decided to take was at the foot of the bed covered with a towel. As soon as the lunch trays came she readied herself waiting till they brought her tray. Then she closed her door ran into the bathroom and stuffed all the towels into the sink, down the toilet and into the shower drain. She held the towels in the shower down with a metal stool flipped upside down. Then after flushing the toilet, she turned all the faucets on full force! Lisa took the sandwich off the tray and tucked it into her roll, leaving her door open. She checked the nurse's desk, no one was there most of them had gone to lunch. She hid and waited for the commotion to begin from the running water.

Soon, someone yelled, "Help!" She heard running and an orderly hollered for someone to get the mops and buckets. Peeking up she saw her chance and pushed the button opening the doors. Out she went as fast as possible. Quickly she slowed her pace to appear that she was just another visitor there. She smiled at anyone she met and simply walked out of *Meade Hospital* as if on her way to her car. She did some quick thinking and decided to get away from the parking lot and onto a side street as soon as she could quicken her pace. 'No telling how long before they realize I'm missing.' Lisa knew they'd hunt for her and that she'd need to stay off the main roads. 'My what a pretty street, what an adventure. I'll see parts of *Meade* I've never been to before.' Lisa carried her small roll of belongings as if it were a purse. 'It's a lovely day and the flowers are so pretty. No hurry, I'm just going for a walk no law against that.' She did in fact appear to be a lady out for a stroll with her hair combed neatly and her clothes chosen carefully for this day. It was 1:30 PM and she'd been gone from the ward since about 12:20. Inwardly Lisa smiled to herself pleased that she'd pulled it off. The sandwich she took was for her supper that night.

Back at the hospital all security guards and nurses knew a Mrs. Lisa Mason was missing. They were all busy checking the entire hospital before calling her family. By quarter to three they'd combed the entire hospital including the lot. When Doctor Simon phoned John and Lisa's house he received no answer. He quickly dialed the other number at Bill and Marcy's.

"Hello, *Mason Haven* may I help you? This is Mrs. Mason."

"This is Doctor Simon calling from *Meade Hospital*. I'm calling to tell you that your daughter-in-law has somehow managed to walk out of here. We've checked the entire area and notified the police to look for her. I'm very sorry, please tell John and I'll call you the minute we find her. She's on foot she couldn't have gone far. We estimate she's only been gone since twelve thirty. Goodbye for now."

CHAPTER 20

It didn't take Lisa long to figure out she had no idea where she was. She'd walked herself into a maze of country homes and had no idea which way to go. As evening closed in she began to wonder where to spend the night. She had no identification purse or money. Hoping for a public park and finding none she chose the corner of a large yard and settled into an area of shrubs and trees where she felt hidden. 'Calm down, spread out your towel and eat the sandwich. Yuck' she thought, 'it doesn't taste good but it's all there is, so eat it.' After eating half she was thirsty and looked around for a faucet. She heard a dog barking and it was getting louder. 'Oh my gosh a dog is coming right for me. Gotta run get away.' She ran as fast as she could out the gate of the fenced yard and waited. The barking stopped; slowly she walked back and peeked in. A large dog was eating the rest of her sandwich. 'Hurry up' she thought 'and leave so I can get what's left of my things.' After the dog left she went back and shook out the towel with exasperation and decided to find another place to spend the night.

As darkness came, she felt more hidden. 'If I can find a street I know it might be safe to walk in the dark. If a car comes I can duck down and hide. First I have to find one though; I'm so tired and feel sick. Keep going Lisa you can do this' she thought. 'I'm coming to the end of the street I entered, at least I think it is. Hmm, turn left or right.' Left she decided and walked some more. Headlights were coming toward her; she quickly went into the shadows and waited. "There" she said aloud, tears of relief came over her as she saw the street sign. 'Old Riverview Road, that leads toward home. Oh well I'll take it at least I know where I am now. Gotta stop and rest, here comes another car.' She backed into the shadows again, this time it was a police car driving slowly. She wondered, 'Are they looking for me? Quite probably! I better be careful, good they're going on by me.' Lisa walked till she thought she couldn't walk anymore. All together she'd probably walked about six miles with all the circling around. She stopped more often now but stayed on the Old Riverview Road only ducking down when a car came near. With a tear stained face and her body screaming for rest she saw a familiar light ahead. It was in the church bell tower; just the sight of it made her sob. Without further thought she struggled toward it. She went around to the back, 'I remember the porch, I can stay the night here.' Lisa spread out the dirty towel and lay down in a ball and fell asleep with her arms wrapped around her stomach.

"Hello" she heard, "Are you all right?" Lisa couldn't get her eyes to focus at first. When she did, she thought she recognized one of the Sisters of the parish.

"Can I help you? Do I know you she asked her?"

Lisa answered with the first thing that came to mind.

"Yes maybe, please can I go inside? I need to see the priest."

"Yes of course, I'll take you to the rectory first and let you freshen up, you'll feel better. Then I'll get Father O'Brien for you." Lisa was scared and confused, "Yes, please" she said, and followed her in. After she was done they went into church, morning Mass was nearly over.

"Sit here, till Mass is over, he'll be happy to see you."

"Thanks Sister" Lisa said, in a short time she heard;

"Well, Lisa Mason is it" Father O'Brien said, smiling benevolently at her. "And what can I do to help you?"

"Please Father hear my confession, and bless me I need healing."

"Yes of course, let's just sit here and be comfortable."

Through sobs Lisa told Father O'Brien how she felt about the twins and that she knew it was wrong but she couldn't seem to help it.

"It's all right Lisa, God has all ready forgiven you," he explained that she was sick, and that God loved her and understood all these things. He blessed her, and gave her Holy Communion.

"Lisa, if you didn't care about the life you carry you wouldn't have found your way here to get help! Now let's go back to the rectory and get you something to eat" he said.

"I'm going to need to phone your family, I hope you won't be angry with me for that. Will you little one?" When he said that, all of the anger within her drained out, she felt all her fatigue at once.

"No" she said, "please call John."

He was there in a few minutes. Time was lost for Lisa; she couldn't comprehend it, but knew she needed help. At least right at this minute she knew it! John was so relieved and happy to see her.

"Everyone has been so worried about you Lisa. Why did you leave?"

"I'm not really sure" she said, "I just had to get out of there, I felt trapped."

"It's going to be all right honey, your mom is on the way here and I will get you released from the hospital. You can see Doctor Simon as an out patient, Okay?"

"Yes, oh John yes please it was awful in there, please never leave me there again."

"I promise, except when the twins arrive we will have to go, but not to that part of the hospital, only the maternity ward. You'll be fine love."

John took her home, Marcy stayed with her till he came back from talking with the doctor and signing the papers to release her. Doctor Simon said she'd be all right at home as long as someone stayed with her at all times. "I'll see her for an hour a week," he said. It was all settled.

Grace arrived and stayed with Lisa and John. When he could be there he was, and Alex, well Alex was fine. He stayed with Bill and Marcy and continued in pre-school. On the days when Lisa was functioning, Marcy brought him over to visit. Over all Lisa improved, however it was clear that she needed psychiatric care. Grace traveled back and forth from *Mason Haven* and home until the twins were born. It just happened that she was in Georgia when Lisa's labor began. She was about a month short of what her doctor hoped for.

* Wednesday, February 3, 1988 *

This particular night, after feeding the horses John left for town. He slipped back into the habit of staying out, a fact that didn't please either of his parents. And with Grace back in Georgia, Lisa was sleeping in the main house. She is in the same room and bed as before she and John married. Her bout with toxemia was no joke! Marcy had Bill move her wedge of foam over to elevate her legs.

At 2:10 AM Lisa woke with gripping pain. Instinctively she wrapped her arms around her stomach to hold and comfort herself. She could see the time by the night-light Marcy put there for her.

'I've got to pee so bad,' she thought as she scooted and rolled to the edge of the bed pitched herself off and aimed toward the bathroom. 'Easy now' she thought, just as she took a step another pain hit. This time she recognized it for what it was. After relieving herself she made her way to Bill and Marcy's room and called.

"Mom, Dad sorry, to wake you but my labor started."

Marcy wasn't asleep anyway and answered her immediately.

"Coming Lisa," she helped her back into bed.

"Just let me get dressed to take you to the hospital and then I'll reach John."

"It's all right Mom, I know John is troubled and it's my fault."

Marcy wouldn't let that go.

"No it isn't Lisa, none of this is your fault. Don't think that for a minute. I need to tend to a few arrangements for Alex and then I'll be right back. Good thing we packed your suitcase last week. I'll phone your parents too."

"Thanks I'd really like them to know even if they can't come up right away. I love you," she said. Marcy's eyes burned with tears as she hurried about doing what was necessary.

John spent the evening at the *Water Trough* tavern with Clarese Lampson, often his habit over the last three months. They closed the bar and then went to her house. That is where he learned that his wife was in labor…The shame he felt was indescribable, but no more than he deserved. Marcy knew which of his friends to call to get the number to reach him. She spared her son nothing.

"John get your sorry ass to the hospital your wife is in labor with your twins!" She slammed the phone down and went directly to Lisa and drove her to the hospital. They arrived at 4:20 AM, had her admitted and into a labor room where she stayed with Lisa until John arrived at 5:00 AM. Without a word of comfort to John, she looked him straight in the eye and said, "I'm going home and tend to Alex and your father!"

Later back at *Meade Hospital*. The lights glared down on Lisa as the team of doctors, and nurses worked to save her. After about seven hours of labor, they rushed her to surgery for an emergency cesarean section. It was 9:15 AM. While monitoring the infants closely, they struggled to stabilize Lisa. Toxemia had taken its toll on her health along with all the stress. Her heart monitor signaled trouble as her blood pressure fluctuated out of control. While the anesthetist adjusted her oxygen flow, Lisa's heart went into arrhythmia, shortly followed by full cardiac arrest.

In the spiritual realm Lee, Cassy's father recalls all of this as if it was yesterday. Incredible! Being able to watch both—as Cassy and Lisa's lives unfold, each on their own journey. I knew Lisa's soul would soon be here safe with the rest of us on the other side. I'll tell her how her life will continue with Cassy's soul in her body. She will be happy to know Alex, John, and the twins will be loved and alright.

"Hurry!" The doctor yelled,
"Get that defibrillator in place…all clear…Hit it!" Nothing…Flat!—
"Try again…—Now—!" Several seconds passed…Finally success! Sighs of relief followed, then a cheer rose in the operating room as Lisa's vitals began to stabilize.

This was the instant of the miracle…Cassy's soul now dwelled in Lisa's body. Her doctors were amazed at the strength with which their patient's heart now exhibited. From the outside she appeared the same. Inside, a different story, oh what a change!
"All right let's get those babies out quickly." Within half an hour two babies were born. Yet to be named, the baby girl was lifted out first, followed by her brother. Both were healthy; Lisa carried her twin's one month short of full term. They weighed five pounds one

ounce, and four pounds five ounces. The baby girl was the heaviest! While the surgical team stitched Lisa, her doctor went out to tell John the good news.

In the unseen world of the spiritual cheers also rang out. An angel and Cassy's father smiled welcoming Lisa's soul home to rest. If only we could see God's face. All knowing eyes with tears of joy. Some day we will know the depth of God's omnipotent love.

John has just been allowed to go in with Lisa, and to see the twins in the nursery. He is extremely happy that Lisa made it through the birth of the twins safely; but had no idea of the change…Lisa is a new woman!
"Honey they are beautiful, wait till you see them. The nurse said she'd bring them in to us in half an hour. Your C-section was complicated by carrying twins, your toxemia, and hard labor." John held Lisa's hand and had the silliest urge to kiss that beautiful mouth of hers. He bent down and kissed her gently and whispered how proud he was of her and the twins who were so perfect.
"Imagine" he said,
"How unusual it is to have twins, a boy and girl twins! We need to talk about names after you rest and sleep. You tell me when you're ready to decide, okay?"
"Yes I will" was all Lisa could manage. 'Lisa's body is going to need rest,' she reminded herself. 'So this is what it feels like to have a baby,—twins, yikes and to be loved by a husband. I can feel the strength of his love, and his touch is—is unlike any touch I've known!'
As John looks into Lisa's face he's thinking, 'there are no thoughts of Clarese in my mind now! The impact of my love for Lisa is so strong and my desire for her never wanes. Not even now, you pervert!' His thoughts are interrupted as the nurse brings in the twins for their first visit with their parents.

"Hello Mr. & Mrs. Mason, here are your beautiful babies. The whole nursery is buzzing about them." She put them both in Lisa's arms and asked,

"Are you going to nurse them?" Without hesitation she said, "Yes."

"Okay then mother, get them started they will need the colostrum for the antibodies it gives them until your milk comes in."

Lisa thought to herself, 'This might be embarrassing in front of John as she positioned her daughter to nurse.' She was amazed that she wasn't,—not a twinge.

"Here John, hold your son till it's his turn to nurse." As this little daughter nursed she looked down at the tiny puckered face and knew the depths of love. Names began floating back and forth in her mind.

"Let's switch them John, here hold your daughter and give me our son." Changing breasts she looked down to a near identical profile and was in awe. 'How precious they are God, I thank you for this gift of life with my whole heart.'

"Hmm, names" she said out loud.

"What do you think?" John was mesmerized and sat silent for a moment or two.

"I think you should have first choice. If I absolutely hate a name you choose I will be honest, but you decide." Lisa wrinkled her brow in concentration.

"How about Susan Marie?"

"For the boy?"

"Now you are being silly, for her of course" she said, and they both laughed. Lisa was enjoying this as sore as her posterior and stomach was.

"I feel neutral about that name it's alright, but it doesn't thrill me either" John said.

"All right, how about Cecilia Lynne Mason, and William Brett Mason?" Now it was John's turn to tease and hesitate.

"Are you sure you like those names?" he asked.

"Well, yes" she said.

"They sound good together with Mason. Don't you like them?"

"Let me think longer," John stalled.

"You said I could name them," Lisa complained. He couldn't keep his smile in any longer.

"I love both names I really do." He was rewarded with one of Lisa's prettiest smiles.

"Can I call her Ceci for short?"

"Absolutely not" she said, and then smiled till he grinned from ear to ear.

CHAPTER 21

Marcy and Bill prepared for their home coming with a thorough cleaning of the house. She saw to it that fresh flowers were on the table and that the baby gifts that were still arriving were stacked in a corner of the living room. There was no spare room this time as when Alex was born. As she finished she said to Bill,

"We need to see if there is a spare dresser for these new clothes. Let's look in the shed later okay?"

"As a matter of fact I've got one in my house I never use" Amos said. He was also there lending a helping hand.

"Great, if one of you can help me, I'll put a fresh coat of paint on it and we can have it ready when they get home tomorrow." Bill and Amos carried it to the house as Marcy went for the paint. Everything was as prepared as they could make it! She stood back cocked her head and admired the results. "Splendid just right" she said smiling!

The young Mason family arrived home with excitement, and joy. Home where love would thrive, and a warm welcome for their two new members. Alex was jumping up and down he was so happy to see them. He handed Lisa a flower that was clutched in his sweet chubby hand. "Momma, I picked it for you" he said. Lisa went to him first giving him a hug, attention he needed, and craved. She was well prepared for her new role as wife and mother; smooth sailing ahead—right! Wrong, the drama is just beginning. It's true that Cassy's soul was prepared for her transition into Lisa's life. Still life's challenges not only continue but also escalate. All that follows into their lives she will cope with in a way that our former Lisa never could have. Even when life's pathway leads us deceptively onto a smooth plane, it never lasts. This is how life is for us all. And Lisa came into the middle of a three-ring circus! After her hospital stay, they returned home to a small two-bedroom house with a four-year-old, and a set of newborn twins. Oh, did I mention there is only one bathroom!

Two weeks later, when John left for work, Lisa looked around and felt like weeping. 'How in the heck am I going to organize this place' she wondered. 'I have so much to get used to that my mind is spinning. No wonder Lisa had problems. That reminds me,' she thought, 'Marcy said that I have an appointment with my doctor week after next, a Doctor Simon.'

"Shoot, I was all ready to courteously fire him," she said with a tongue in cheek smile. 'I might need him after all! Dang it, settle down girl and get a grip on yourself. Alex is at pre-school the twins are napping now is your chance to settle in.' First she went over to her dresser, sat down and looked at herself really looked at herself. "Hello Lisa" she said to this pretty woman. 'I am sort of pretty even if I do say so. As Cassy I never felt this feminine or sexy. I love the way John keeps looking at me.' A slow smile crossed her face as goose bumps rose on her arms. She looked into all the drawers learning where everything was. Picking up a brush she began pulling it through her thick wavy hair, she couldn't help but admire the shine. Lisa sat up very straight and noticed her womanly curves liking them. Standing up, she turned side ways and studied her profile. 'Hmm pretty slim for just having twins.'

"Ouch," she said out loud, without realizing it she'd been holding her stomach in and the staples were pulling. 'That's what I get for admiring myself' she thought with a wry smile. 'Tomorrow I go to the doctor for my first postnatal check up and to have the staples out. None too soon either they are beginning to itch, but that is a good sign of healing.'

Next she went through the closet and checked over her clothes, John's, and each of the children's. It seemed to her that there wasn't a shortage of anything for any of them. 'Lisa I love you for taking such care of everything, how dear' she thought as she wrapped her arms around herself in a hug. She looked up at the sky when she went out in the yard to admire the garden. "Thanks God, and thanks to you Lisa" she said, and meant it with her whole heart. 'Oops, there are my little ones, it's time for changing and feeding. I enjoy feeding them' she thought as she hurried in to them.

John was still taking lunch with his dad, mom, and Amos to help ease her busy schedule. 'I appreciate the help' she thought, 'but miss seeing him, he certainly isn't hard to look at. Sleeping with him is like heaven, no demands just the intimacy of sleeping together and affection without obligation for sexual relations—yet! I already feel love for him both as a person and-I-know that my body yearns for his. Well Lisa, you're just being honest with yourself. There is one part that I am wondering about however, technically I am a virgin. I mean I feel like one because as Cassy I'd never been with a man. Oh well, I was told I'd be given all I need to know so I will just need to trust.' Lisa enjoyed daydreaming about her new life!

What Lisa didn't know was how they hadn't been close in a sexual way, yet they had the children together. The twins at least! She knew some of Lisa's horrendous childhood. She knew that Alex was not John's biological son. 'He was bless him, a child as the result of rape. Alex is the perfect example of how God takes something bad, and changes it into a gift of profound goodness.'

She reminded her-self, and pondered all these facts often to familiarize herself.

'I know that I have come well equipped to cope with the present and function well as wife and mother. I will relish it with grace and most of all with love. All will be good, I can feel it in my heart.'

Lisa didn't know about Clarese Lampson yet...That was to be a battle in the future for her. Right now there was more than enough to do just cooking and cleaning. Little Alex was such a good helper a big brother. "How I love that little cutie," she said right out loud. 'Almost time for him to be home,' Marcy was taking him and picking him up. 'More help, what a dream of a mother-in-law!'

That night after John helped her with cleanup he said he'd be home later, that he was going out for awhile. Lisa didn't think too much of it and automatically leaned over to receive his kiss. She wasn't disappointed for John was naturally affectionate as a person.

"Alright John, we'll all be here at home—just waiting for you!" She said this with a sweet voice, but with an edge to it. Inside John's head there was confusion and inner turmoil. He was used to the Lisa who was so accepting of whatever he did unless she was having one of her bouts with psychosis. 'Since our twins were born she seems—different, better and happier. That is great and I'm so glad. Still it is a puzzle.' These were the thoughts that ran through his head as he left for another tryst with Clarese. Funny how she had become much like the beer he drank too much of, a habit!

With the stitches out Lisa began to move with more freedom and felt better. "John" she said, "would you like more breakfast?" He rocked his chair back and smiled at her, "No thanks that's plenty. Gotta get to work soon, we have a hay delivery today."

"Wait a minute, I have a question, won't take a minute."

"Sure, go ahead" John said.

"I think it's time we think about a trip south to see my folks, Sally, and the senior Windsor's. Time to introduce them to the twins especially my parents. What do you think, could we?"

"Hmm, I think you're right! I'll talk with dad and Amos about it later and see when we can get away for a few days, how's that sound?"

"Sounds great and thanks, see you tonight. Oh, and we're having steak and salad for supper so I won't start till you get home except for the baked potatoes."

"Yum" he said, as the screen door slammed shut. Lisa watched him go and adored the sight of him with that silly sweet dog at his heels.

With the weather warm, and summer nearly here it was perfect for the drive. All went well on the trip south to *Windsor Stock Farm*. Lisa was a little uneasy about being with her parents and seeing Sally, 'oh never mind' she thought; 'it'll be just fine.' Jeb and Grace heard them pulling in and came out to greet them. Sally came down from the Windsor's home where she spent a great deal of time these days. Both Mr. and Mrs. Windsor were frail needing nursing and constant care. Trips back and forth to doctor's appointments kept them both busy, and also Grace and Sally busy helping them.

"Hello" Lisa yelled as she opened the door. They were driving the new Chevy Suburban they'd picked out together in *Meade* last week. The car was too small now for all the car seats and the baby equipment needed these days.

"Hello Lisa, John, Alex, and who have we here? They are adorable, both Cecilia, and Willie. Give your mom a hug Lisa, you too John. How we've missed you kids, come here Alex and let grandma hug you."

"Coming Grandma," he went running into her arms.
"Me too" Jeb chimed in as Sally began peeking in at the babies.
"Hi Alex" Sally said. "Is this your new little brother and sister?"
"Uh hu, and their names are Cecilia, and Willie!"
"Momma," he called, "can I take the babies out of the car seats?"
"Yes, Alex but I need to help you sonny." They all admired the twins and the Suburban too in that order and then remembered to tell Alex what a good big brother he was.

"John, how does it handle on the road, do you like it?" Jeb asked as they went to the barns to look at the new horses and talk over the latest business.
"Yeah, I really like this machine, it's a great family vehicle, but I miss the Malibu's punch!"

"Come in y'all," Grace said, as she led the way holding little Cecilia, Sally was holding Willie. 'I'm enjoying this' Lisa thought. "They are adorable both of them, nearly as handsome as you Alex," Grace said. That made him smile.
"I think they're precious," he said, parroting what he'd heard his gramma Marcy say.
"That's what Marcy says every day she sees the three of them," Lisa explained.
"Well they are" Grace said.
"How are you coping with all this added excitement Lisa?"
"Fine in fact I feel better and happier than I have in years."
"Well bless my soul, our prayers are being answered, there is an angel for our Lisa after all," Grace said. Little did she know how true this was!
"You know Lis, you really do look better," Sally chimed in.
"That news really makes me happy, and it's high time too."
"What's high time?" Alex wanted to know.

"Oh that's an expression that means something should have happened sooner!"

"Well then" Alex said, "It's high time I had a cookie."

They had a good chuckle over that.

"He sure is a quick one" Sally said as she handed him a cookie off the kitchen table.

"Yes, he is" Lisa agreed, "Can you believe it, he'll start school next September!"

"Where does the time go," Grace said wistfully.

When Lisa and Grace took Alex up to visit Mr. and Mrs. Windsor it was plain to see this could possibly be the last time that they'd see him. Both had a weakened heart condition which made it difficult for them to get around. They loved Alex and doted on him, which pleased both Lisa and Grace. When they were getting ready to leave for home Lisa took him back to say goodbye. It was a picture she would remember for a long time.

As John loaded the Suburban with their gear Lisa said her good byes and gave hugs to them. It was easy to love them and she felt the bond strongly. "Bye Sally, write when you can but be sure and phone too." Sally looked down at the ground so Lisa wouldn't see her tears.

"I will Lisa, I promise and come back when you can." Lisa went over and gave her a quick hug and then got in the seat to go. John said,

"Hey all of you, please come up for Christmas this year you too Sally. It will be a big one for us with the twins old enough to have fun and Alex always has fun!"

"Thanks John, we'll have to see, but that sounds great we'll sure try to make it. Keep in close touch please."

"We will, and you do the same, we love y'all—bye."

Lisa looked over at John as they drove out saying,

"It's sure strange coming here." As John pulled onto the highway turning toward Kentucky he said, "tell you what Lisa, it doesn't feel strange heading for home! I love your parents and I'm fond of Sally but I really love our home." Lisa let a few minutes pass before saying,

"I know what you mean I feel the same, Kentucky is home."

The following week they had an unexpected phone call from Jeb. He was glad John answered,

"Hi John, I have some sad news, Mrs. Windsor died in her sleep last night. It was not a surprise really but we feel sad about it, I'd appreciate it if you'd tell Lisa."

"No problem Jeb glad to, and you'll be happy to know that our Lisa is coping very well with everything these days."

"Great" Jeb said, "No reason for you to come down for the funeral. We'll sit in for you so to speak and we'll be in touch. Talk soon, bye John."

"Bye Jeb, and thanks."

Within three weeks of her death, Mr. Windsor had a massive heart attack following his wife into the here after. Grace phoned telling them about this final loss of the dear old couple.

After both funeral services were over and the will was read there was surprising good news to share. Grace called and Lisa answered.

"Hi Mom, what's going on?"

"You won't believe it, but it's true. The senior Windsor's left the whole *Windsor Stock Farm* to Alex. It is held in trust until he's of age and we are to take care of it for him till then. They were generous Lis, isn't that great!"

"Yes it is, Wow I'm so pleased for Alex it will secure his future."

"We are too, and Lis, they left your father and I one hundred thousand dollars they said for faithful service."

"Oh Mom, I'm so glad you and Dad deserve that, you've worked so hard over the years for them."

"Hang on Sally wants to talk to you for a minute."

"Sure, okay." John was pleased about the news too. Just think he thought, 'both farms joined together in the same family!'

"Hi Sally how are you?"

"Couldn't be better, the Windsor's also left me a generous gift, enough for me to put a down payment on a small house."

"Sally, that is super, will you continue to work there?"

"No, I made up my mind to quit work here after they passed on. I want to get my nursing degree. I'm enrolled in college for the fall semester right here in town, and will still live here with your folks."

"Sally, I couldn't be more pleased for you, go girl! That is really super, stay in touch please. Bye for now."

"Bye Lisa."

CHAPTER 22

After her appointment with Doctor Simon she had a much better understanding of Lisa's past life. Listening to him review with her gave a deep appreciation of Lisa's spirit. Sensing his respect, and fatherly love, she immediately liked Doctor Simon.

"Well, what is this I hear from your OB.-GYN. you're doing much better?" His smile warmed her, and it was obvious he was interested in all aspects of her life.

"It's true, I really do feel stronger and better and I thank you, for all of your help. With your approval, I think the time has come to extend the frequency between our visits, what do you think?" Doctor Simon swiveled his chair more squarely toward her and said, "yes Lisa I agree, as long as you'll phone the office and make an appointment with me if anything changes, or if you feel bad, will you do that?"

"Yes, I certainly will."

"I'd like you to come in at least once a year, I will truly miss you. So, unless I hear from you, I'll see you next summer sometime."

"Of course I will," she said.

"Thanks again for all the help you've given to me over the last four years, you're a good friend."

"I assure you it was a pleasure young lady. I am sincerely happy you are better. These are the times in my profession when I feel it's all worth while, so I thank you. If you're in the area shopping I would like it if you just stopped by to say hello."

"Thanks Doctor Simon, I'll do that!"

While he was happy with Lisa's remarkable recovery, he was equally puzzled being curious by nature. In all the many years of his psychiatry practice he had never experienced a case like Lisa Mason's. This had him totally intrigued. He already planned to do extensive research regarding this, and considered her case most unusual! He hoped to write a comprehensive medical research paper, and submit it to both the Psychiatric Medical Board, and the AMA. Consequently he had a duel reason in wanting to stay in contact with her, and to observe the progression of her continued recovery.

When Lisa returned home she stopped by the main house to pick up the twins and visit Marcy.

"Hi Mom, were they good for you?" Marcy beamed at her; she clearly enjoyed the time spent with them.

"Let's see, Cecilia didn't cry at all, and Willie only cried once but quit as soon as the bottle went into his mouth. I have to make an excuse for him though because I fed Cecilia first!"

"It's so quiet, are they napping, must be," she giggled at her own question. "Yes for about half an hour. Let's let them sleep for now" Marcy said, "so we can talk. There are two or three things I want to talk with you about. Would you like a cold drink?"

"No thanks I'm not thirsty," Lisa said relaxed and ready to listen.

"First and rather important regarding your house and this one. I wanted to talk to you first, see what you think before either of us asks John. It always concerns the wife first I believe. How would you feel about switching homes? You John and the children move here, and we'll move into our old first home. Bet you didn't know that was our first home together. It makes sense to me; we're getting older and would like less to keep up. Besides it'll be kinda romantic to be back there. Bill's parents used to live here when they were alive and we only moved in here after they retired. So what do you think, would you like more room for the kids?" Lisa took it all in listening attentively.

"Yes, if John agrees, I think it would be great if you and Bill are sure. You've done so much for us already."

"Believe me we're sure Lisa, we've talked about it and looked forward to it. We'll be free to do more traveling as John takes on more responsibility with the business."

"Okay then" Lisa said, "it's almost lunch time and I want to begin fixing John's lunches, and also take Alex to pre-school from now on. I am feeling great and so appreciate all of the help you've given me. Thanks with all my heart Mom. "You're welcome Lisa, I was happy to help."

"Next week I go for my final doctors visit and will take the twins in for their checkup too. Gosh there is so much to tell you, Doctor Simon agreed I don't need to see him for a year unless I should need to." Marcy smiled saying, "that's the best news of all. Oh, and before I forget, the night before the twins were born you left your rosary here. I kept forgetting to give it to you so here before I forget again," handing it to her. Lisa put it in her pocket a little surprised even though she knew the family was Catholic, and now she was too. "Thanks, and we need to see about having the twins baptized don't we," Lisa said.

"Yes you beat me to it, I was going to ask you about that. Alex was what, about six months I think a little older but we were so busy then. Would you like me to make the arrangements with the church?"

"Thanks but I'll take care of it, and I want to run it past John first." Smiling Marcy said, "good idea, I'll help you get the babies up, and then get lunch on the table for Bill and Amos. Lisa I made extra sandwiches won't you take two of these for John's lunch it'll save you time today?"

"Thanks so much Mom, it will help I am a little late! I will speak to John about moving and also about the twins baptism then get back to you about the date." As they put the sleepy twins into the Suburban Lisa thanked Marcy again saying she'd let her know the date later by phone.

When Lisa got home John was just arriving for lunch. "Hi honey he said is lunch about ready?"

"Sure is thanks to Mom. Here she made the sandwiches today. I'll get you a glass of milk and be right back. We need to talk, as soon as I put these babes in the playpen."

"Guess what, your parents want to change homes with us and we could use the extra room, how do you feel about it?"

"If you would like it Lisa I think it'd be great. I know that they used to live here where we are now."

"I know, she was telling me about that how it would be easier for them with less up keep as they begin to retire from full time work."

"Sounds great honey, we can talk more about it tonight, was there anything else love?"

"Yes, about the twins baptism. If you agree I'll go ahead and phone the parish today and arrange to have our little muffins baptized."

"It's time we thought about that, thanks for thinking of it and for arranging it. I need to get back to work, talk to you tonight." Lisa gave him a hug and kiss as he ran out the door. "Bye see you later love." It was time to feed the twins, and then put them back in the playpen while she called the church.

"Hello, this is Lisa Mason."

"Hello, how are all of you? This is Father O'Brien."

"We're all fine thanks, I was just calling to make arrangements for our twins baptism."

"Good, let's see we have just about any date open you'd like, when would you like it done?"

"How about September 29th it's our wedding anniversary, would that be all right?"

"That will be fine, tell John and his folk's hello for me. Hope to see you all before then of course. Let's see Alex will be four this coming December, time sure goes in a hurry."

"Yes it does, hardly seems possible that we've been married four years the end of September."

"That's right," he said "How would you like to have your wedding vows renewed at that time, I do that you know?"

"Oh Father O'Brien, I would like that very much, thanks talk to you soon."

Lisa smiled as she strapped Cecilia and Willie into their car seats to go get Alex. 'What a great idea, it's perfect, then I'll really feel married to this man.' When she got home she called Marcy and told her the baptism was set for their anniversary September 29th and that Father would bless their marriage with renewal of their vows. Marcy was so happy saying she'd mark it down on the calendar.

When she wasn't busy with the children, she poked around and hunted through their papers, wedding certificate, Alex's baptismal papers, and also found her bible and special mementos tucked inside that would help her learn more about her new found church, and faith.

'I remember my mom telling me about her baptism. Let's see, she said a preacher came through their camp one summer and did a mass river baptism and that included both of my parents. I was baptized at the church my mom and I attended in New York long ago.' She smiled wistfully remembering it. 'One day if possible perhaps we can vacation at *Berry Cove* New York. I would like to know that my mom is all right. Don't worry God I haven't forgotten my promise not to tell.' Without warning tears spilled out as she remembered the times they spent together. Inwardly she whispered, 'I love you mom.' Then she let the thought go and began fixing supper.

"Alex would you like to help me set the table?" He came running in from the bedroom,

"Yes very much what part can I do huh?"

"Let's see love, how about if you put out the spoons, forks, and napkins." He ran over to the cupboard to get the napkins.

"Momma how many?" This was a nightly ritual,

"Only three one for you, one for me, and one for your daddy."

John came in with a grin and a slam of the screen door.

"Hello, how's my Lisa, Alex, Cecilia, and Willie doing tonight?"

John stayed home and they talked late that night about all that had taken place that day.

That following week, Lisa and the twin's eight-week check up went well, Lisa began having thoughts of love and romance with John. She prepared herself mentally, or at least convinced herself she was, and dreamed of it over and over. In fact this night she was prepared to hurry through supper and put the kids down early. Just as she was putting Alex into bed, John poked his head around the corner looking all spruced up. 'Great,' she thought, 'he has the same idea as me.'

"Hey honey" he smiled,

"Thought I'd go out and have a few beers, I'll see you later tonight." Lisa didn't miss a beat, she kissed Alex as she always did and said,

"I think you should say goodnight to your son first then we'll talk in the living room—please."

'Oops' John thought, 'I think maybe I'm in trouble.'

"Alright honey, be right in."

'Shoot, last time she had her postnatal checkup I remember what happened shortly there after. I don't want to be anywhere near her. That's all we need right now another baby. It's not my fault she's so fertile!'

When he came in she had her back to him looking out the side window. He went over and put his arms around her waist hugging her.

"What's wrong sweetheart?"

"I was hoping you'd stay home tonight. The doctor said I am very healthy now."

'Oh God,' John groaned inwardly, 'she sounds hurt'.

"I'm so glad you are sweetheart and the twins too. I was just wanting to unwind with the guys and have a few beers," he lied.

"All right then, tell you what, you go ahead, we can't both go, I didn't arrange for a baby sitter so you just go! But, next time, I'm going with you. I haven't been out one night nor ridden a horse or done anything with you alone in ages."

John was stunned, absolutely shocked.

"Lisa, I'm sorry I had no idea you felt that way." She turned around then, looked up at his face, riveting his eyes to hers as she spoke.

"You also never asked me how I felt. You could have asked your wife for a date you know!"

"I would love to ride with you when ever Mom will watch the kids, shoot I'll take you with me anytime anywhere. I'm so proud to be your husband," and he meant it clear down to his boots.

"All right then, how about tomorrow night provided Mom can sit the kids? I want to meet all your friends both men, and women!" John's mouth fell open.

"Close your mouth John" she said, "did you think I was so crazy I didn't—"

"Now hold on woman, I don't know who you've been talking to but there's only Clarese Lampson at the *Water Trough* tavern, and she used to work here at the farm."

"John, I was only going to say that I knew women went to taverns too! Now who the hell is Clarese Lampson? Just how friendly are you two? Never mind don't even answer that. You go ahead, go out tonight but remember—tomorrow night it's my turn!"

If John had had a way to crawl out the door without loosing face he would have. Instead he said, "I'm sorry Lisa honestly. I'll be home early."

"Don't hurry, and don't worry I won't be waiting up she said!"

'Shit' John thought climbing into the cab of his pickup my knees feel strange. A new experience for him. 'No woman's ever had this effect on me before. I always feel like I'm in control. That's what eats at my insides, Lisa makes me loose focus!' He turned on the radio turned up the volume and rolled down the windows driving faster than usual. When he parked he saw Amos's old beat up Ford pickup, and Clarese's car. Walking in he noticed the usual crowd was there.

"Hi Amos, when you've won that pool game, I'd like to talk." Amos took his time before answering and finished a straight shot scoring.

"Sure John see ya in a bit." Clarese gave him a dirty look for his insult of her pool ability! She smiled inwardly though and thought of later when she'd have him alone-she assumed.

"Hey Phil, give me a beer, yeah thanks the usual." John took his beer and sat down alone in the corner and sipped it watching Amos and Clarese play pool.

When the game was over Clarese moved to the bar and talked to the men bantering as she always did. Amos brought his beer, and sat across from him.

"What the hell's eating at you John? You look like a bear just ripped out your guts." He looked up at Amos for a few seconds before answering:

"It's Lisa!"

"What'd she do, that little bit of a woman, knock the wind out of ya?"

"Yes she did, but it wasn't her fault. I panicked, and thought she knew about Clarese by something she said. I interrupted her, and said something I shouldn't have, I let her know about Clarese." She said, "I don't want to know anymore about it." John looked pale!

"Oh man" Amos said. "Is she mad?"

"That's the funny part, not that I could tell, she just said tomorrow night it was her turn. She wants to come here with me and meet everyone including Clarese!"

"Well then John, that's just what I'd do—if I was you of course! Say, what you going to do about Clarese?"

"What's there to do? I figure I'll introduce her as a friend who used to work at the farm. You know Clarese, she knows everyone, and she is a friend." Both Amos and John smiled with that comment.

"Tell you what Amos, I was sort of hoping you'd ah-take Clarese off my hands—so to speak. How do you feel about that?"

"Dang man, like I was picking up where I left off about a year or so ago; and damned glad to do it!"

"Thanks Amos, see you in the morning, I'm going home." He just looked at John with a grin and said,

"Shoot John, that's what I'd do."

CHAPTER 23

Lisa was awake staring at the ceiling when she heard John drive in. She rolled over and looked at the clock, only 11:30. 'Dang' she thought, 'he did come home early!' She turned toward the wall and pretended to be sleeping, listening to the soft sounds. John undressing, slipping off one boot then the other, near silence a shuffling sound clothes rustled, fell to the floor. A bare foot pushed them over toward the wall then kicked them onto a chair for morning. They both slept the night somewhat restless.

Last nights talk with John was just the catalyst Lisa needed to motivate her. After he left for work she phoned and made arrangements for all the children to stay the night with gramma and grampa until time for Alex to go to pre school tomorrow. It was all set and Marcy didn't say a word just smiled at her.

"I'll bring them over at 5:30 if that's all right," Lisa said.

"Sure we'll enjoy our visit with them, have fun Lisa."

"I plan to," she said.

When John came in from work Lisa was dressing.

"Hi honey," she said. "Ready for a night out with me?" John just stared at her in her low cut black bra and skimpy panties; he took a deep breath and said, "Sure am! Give me time enough to shower and dress then out to supper and an evening with my love." Lisa liked the sound of that. They took his truck as she preferred and went for burgers and fries, also her request. Then to the *Water Trough Tavern* around 9:00 o'clock. When they came in all heads turned to look, many had never seen Lisa. For a moment or two there was silence.

"Howdy you two join the fun," Amos said. He and Clarese were dancing, so they joined them on the floor and danced too. It was Saturday night; they had live music playing. Above the beat of music Lisa said:

"Hi Amos who's your friend?" He spun her around and said this here's my friend Clarese."

"Hello Clarese," glad to meet you, I've heard about you from John and feel as though I know you." She didn't know what to make of that comment but said, "Hi Lisa, I'm glad to meet you too, she lied. Lisa looked spectacular and it wasn't lost on anyone least of all on Clarese. She was wearing a peasant style blouse in black silk with embroidery in delicate white flowers around the neck and black jeans belted in showing her curvy figure. Lisa danced gracefully even in western boots.

Both John and Lisa were having fun; each sipped just one beer for the evening. They seemed lost in each other and Lisa felt herself wanting to do things she'd never even thought of doing before. As they danced at the edge of the floor she reached up and breathed in his ear, "I love you John." That had a rather profound effect on him. He held her tighter and kissed her full on the mouth for a few moments, which seemed much too short for Lisa. She felt dizzy from it thinking, 'get a grip girl, this isn't the time to fall apart.'

He whispered, "I worship you Lisa, your love means the world to me, let's go home—now!"

Reaching back she slid her hands into both his hip pockets with just enough pressure to push him closer to her. Lisa said, "Yes, let's go home!"

Neither turned on a light going in. The moon supplied enough to see them to their room. Standing together without need of words Lisa slowly undressed John, one boot then the other and then his shirt as she kissed his back, arms chest and then his fingers. 'I can't believe this is happening' he thought, then all his thoughts vanished. He surrendered to the moment. He leaned to kiss her sweet tempting lips; she stopped him with her finger. "No, remember me first please." Her voice was filled with yearning and a woman's passion. It seemed passion held in check for a lifetime. He said nothing savoring, cherishing the feel, and wanting her. Lisa could scarcely breath so intense was her fire with the feel of him. She unbuttoned his jeans, pulling them off. Sliding onto the floor she removed each sock and kissed the tops of his feet. John was emotionally shattered by this tender show of her love.

"Now my turn, I want your mouth" he whispered. He lifted her onto the bed and caressed her with clothes on sliding his hand slowly, tenderly down her neck and inside her blouse as he kissed the mouth he adored. John teased the corners of her lips with his tongue then slid it inside feeling the silken texture of her. Lisa moaned audibly, answering his kiss with her tongue. Just for a second it occurred to her 'you've never done this before' then all thought vanished as John continued his pursuit of slowly undressing her. Each touch each kiss raising their passion higher assuring her of his love. He led her into the shower and they bathed each other and felt the union of spirits joining even before their bodies came together. The wait served their love and enticed their skin as they dried each other.

Lisa made the first move dropping the towels to the floor as she wrapped her body around his. John took her in his arms and carried her to bed. Without another word they pleasured each other to climax, rested and made love again. They slept together entwined, swaddled in their sheets of love making, awakening to kiss and make love again. That morning was sheer bliss for them both. Lisa finally knew what it meant to love, to give her-self completely to John, and to return love holding nothing back. John, well he felt he'd been made love to for the first time. Quite a thought for a man of his experience. The completeness of her love was worth every minute of the wait. Lisa is well!

The weeks flew by, and the move was nearly complete with both factions of the Mason family exhausted from it all including Amos who always helped them. Both were making the adjustment and settling in. Busy lives give their own reward, satisfaction of hard work done well! The entire Mason clan was sleeping soundly as they settled into their new routines in their different homes. Each women claiming their space, making it uniquely theirs in décor. Bill and Marcy were enjoying their newfound freedom in retirement. Now he could show up as advisor, helper and engage himself in all parts of the business, an experience that gave him satisfaction, and joy. Some days he and Marcy just enjoyed sleeping in and having a leisurely breakfast recalling their early days at *Mason Haven*.

On September 29th 1988 John and Lisa's 4th anniversary, the twins were baptized, Cecilia Lynne Mason and William Brett Mason. Father O'Brien blessed John and Lisa's marriage in a renewal of their wedding vows as the family gathered together including Jeb, Grace, Sally and Amos. All in all it was a busy month with Alex already in kindergarten and loving it. Jeb and Grace came up a few days early, together the ladies planned and ordered a buffet to be served on the lawn in front of the main home. "Isn't this a perfect and happy day"

Grace said to Marcy. "Our joy is really complete now seeing our children happy together and having Lisa feeling good, that is a gift."

"Listen to the men talk," Marcy said to them. "It's typical I suppose the women here reminiscing, and the men over there." Lisa smiled saying,

"And what are they talking about? What else, business-again!"

"Before we know it the holidays will be here, and then Alex turns five years old right after that on the 30th, followed by the twins 1st birthday in February. The years pass quickly," Lisa added. Bill asked for everyone's attention saying, "Here here," lifting his glass, "a toast to both families and to our future health, and happiness." This was another day for them to tuck away in their memories as happy. It was appreciated more keenly contrasted with all the families' grief over the years. John and Bill both took photos with their new video camcorder.

During the transition of moving Lisa talked to both John and his parents about possibly up dating their computer for the business. They agreed it would be a good investment. Marcy had always kept the books with Bill's help. Now Lisa was doing it with John's. It took time spent with Marcy teaching Lisa, and sharing all the records both old and the present. Showing her how the program worked and so forth. With the new PC it would be streamlined, more efficient a real time saver, they both enjoyed the learning. Marcy was impressed with Lisa's natural ability with book keeping. She learned fast and was a whiz with the computer.

Together the two women poured over the old black leather ledgers as far back as 1891. They appreciated the history as well as the carefully recorded penmanship by the early Mason's.

"The men and women who began the Thoroughbred breeding and racing business at *Mason Haven* way back then were good at what they did" Marcy said. "It has quite a history and is a real legacy for the children. Look Lisa, at the old family bible all of the genealogy is kept in here, I've added Cecilia and Willie's names next to Alex's. We need to preserve it all for them."

"They will no doubt all go to college, and may choose another career completely" Lisa said. Marcy smiled at her daughter-in-law agreeing.

"Yes, it's quite possible. Everything ends someday, still I can't help but hope one of them will choose to carry it on."

"Yes, I feel the same" Lisa said.

They enjoyed the holidays together and celebrated the children's birthdays. Another year gone by as John and Lisa celebrated their 5th wedding anniversary while the senior Mason's watched the children. Even the twins now toddlers were talking and it was a joy to listen to them form sentences like Alex had. Even though they were twins Lisa said, "please let's not dress them alike." Even as babies she dressed them different. John and his parents respected that wish too.

"After all" she said, "They are individuals and I want to always honor their different personalities and celebrate that."

John took Lisa on a trip to Toronto Canada for a week of relaxation. What a celebration their anniversary was with luxury gifts from the family. They flew up, rented a car and enjoyed the sights at Niagara Falls, and Lake Ontario. The luxury suite they stayed in at the hotel made Lisa and John's mouths drop open. That part of the trip was a gift from Bill and Marcy. The weather was ideal in late September. Love ruled their waking and sleeping. They feasted more on each other than the sumptuous meals they were served there.

The day before they left, they hiked into dense forest in an area where the trees and wind reigned supreme. Wearing comfortable clothes they took a picnic lunch and blanket with them. The peace of nature, and its' silence filled them, they were alone.

He said, "this is like being the only people on earth."

Lisa smiled, "like 'Adam and Eve' John?" He turned to look at her with that special smile he gave only to her.

"Yes Lisa, just like Adam and Eve come here you." Without preamble he drew her to him and kissed her with all the tenderness and passion he felt at that moment. As she returned his kiss, he began undressing and soon they were wrapped in each other's arms of love. He kissed her nipples until they stood rigid under his lips and fingers, she in turn moved her hands along his chest and down kissing his stomach lower, then lower. She licked John's thighs and kissed him in all his most sensitive places as he moaned with the pleasure she gave him. John took his time kissing Lisa's body with passion caressing her groin until she begged him not to stop. They were one with nature, one with each other. She took his strength fully into her until both were satisfied and spent in love. No two people were more perfectly mated for each other, their bodies fit like matching puzzle pieces. These private moments sustained them, and forever were cherished all their days.

They arrived home to autumn weather, cold wet and with lots of work ahead. Both felt ready to handle anything that came their way.

CHAPTER 24

They had a harsh winter and it wasn't over yet with snow on the ground in April 1990. The horses were feeling buzzed with the high winds and needed riding. Mid morning found Bill home nursing the flu, John and Amos were short handed. Several workers were out sick, and those they had were already exercising horses on the track or on lunge lines. Several of the mares hadn't foaled yet and needed to be taken out. This was a day when they needed twice the hours. John gave Lisa a call at the house,

"Honey what are the chances you can lend us a hand today with the horses I'll explain when you get down here?"

"Good, Lisa said, the twins are in preschool till 2:00 and Alex gets out of school at 2:30."

"Give me long enough to see if mom can pick them up for us and watch them. Then I'll stick with you till quitting time." Marcy was glad to get out of the house and see the kids. Lisa hurried over to the barn dressed for riding.

"Hi John I've been itching to ride it's been over a week."

"Saddle up Tuesday, she's over due with Warrior's foal, and really full of herself today. The ride may bring on her labor, she's a pretty mare fine boned, and long legs, a perfect mare for him. Warrior's all ready saddled; we can take them on the north trail up toward the lake and back. Then home for lunch, and take out a few more if you want."

"I'd like to do some work with the foals too" she said, "if time allows they can always use training on halter and lead."

"Yes Lis, and there's one I'd especially like you to work with, a big bay stud colt. He could use a womans lighter hand he's real touchy."

"Yeah I'd like to try working with him. Where is he?"

"He's in the small paddock at the other end of the barn in with the chestnut filly." Working with horses was natural for Lisa and keenly felt within her spirit. A gift she was given and as close to being born to it as anyone could get.

"Ready Lisa?" John asked,

"Yes, let's go you lead out." With a cold wind at their backs they headed out with Warrior in front. Lisa loved looking at him, John sat a horse like the professional he was, straight and as if he were part of that magnificent stud.

"Easy Tuesday, steady girl," she said.

"Boy John, you weren't kidding this little mare is wired with electricity!"

"I warned you honey just keep a steady rein and she'll settle down." Lisa patted her neck and soothed her with her voice. Tuesday had a sweet disposition, and Lisa was enjoying the crisp air and the ride with John. Warrior was wearing a tie down to keep him from tossing his head too high.

"I hate to use this tie down on him Lisa, but I think he needs it today." The ground had patches of snow and the landscape was breath taking with the evergreens covered in it, and ice glistening on the elm and maple trees.

"How's she doing Lisa?"

"Calmer" she said.

"Let's head back to the barn, it's nearly noon and the others need to be taken out." Lisa turned the mare and headed toward home. They went in for lunch after drying the horses off and putting them into their box stalls. Amos worked drying the others down, they all worked up a sweat.

"Want a bowl of soup John? I'm having some it sounds good."

"Yes, Lisa give me some too, have any crackers? Yes, sounds good to me too, there's coffee left."

"Good" John said, "I'll pour us both a mug."

As she was filling the bowls from the pot on the stove Lisa said, "go ahead and start; I'm calling the folks to see how your Dad's feeling."

"Okay, good idea honey."

"He says he's doing better John, and that your mom's anxious to leave and get the kids already and it's only 12:30." They both laughed about that.

"It's great that she is enjoying being gramma that much, she loves them so much" Lisa said.

"Yes, we're blessed to have both their help. Well, let's get back to work woman, we've got horse's to ride and work!"

"Yes we do, I'll race you to the barn" and she took off running with John and Tag on her heels. Amos had two more saddled and ready to go.

"We'll be taking the same route and we'll be back around 3:00 or before Amos," John told him.

"All right boss man" as they grinned at each other.

"We should be about caught up, then we can work the young'uns for a while. See you later!"

"See you Amos," Lisa yelled as they rode off in the same direction as before. "It's getting colder," she said, "it also looks like we might have more snow tonight."

John looked at the sky and nodded. He agreed.

"I put on a pot roast, potatoes and onions for supper in the slow cooker this morning. It'll be all ready except for the biscuits when we get in."

"Sounds like I'm a lucky man" he said as Lisa smiled at him. They were walking the horses back side by side to cool them down.

"Damn we're blessed aren't we Lisa." Knowing it was a statement not a question. She simply said, "yes we are. Truly beyond my wildest dreams." She'd no sooner said it and she felt a chill. She shivered and pulled her jacket collar close.

Shortly after they heard a motor. It was the pickup coming toward them and Amos was driving. He rolled down the window and yelled;

"Lisa, John your mom and the children have been in an accident!"

"How bad" they both yelled.

"Don't know, but your Dad is waiting for you to go with him, take the truck, I'll take the horses back to the barn. Please phone me soon as you know anything."

"Amos" Lisa yelled, please turn off the crock-pot, in the kitchen and eat the dinner that's in it tonight.

"Thanks Missy," I will. 'God' Lisa thought, 'what odd things come to mind in a crisis.' They ran to the pickup. John drove faster than Lisa could ever remember. "Pray for them John" she said.

"I already am he answered!"

The drive to the hospital was agony for them. Bill asked John to drive; his nerves were so bad. He, being the oldest and least self-conscious prayed out loud. John had difficulty concentrating on the road his worry was so intense. Lisa was praying the rosary to her self without one; by now she didn't need one to know the prayers, adding her own spontaneously as well.

Bill broke the silence just before John pulled into the driveway.

"I phoned the church," he said.

"Father O'Brien is meeting us here."

"Dad and Lisa, get out at the door I'll meet you inside in a second." It didn't take John long to park and run full stride into the emergency entrance.

'They are both already gone inside the depths of the hospital' he thought; odd what runs through the mind. He asked the first nurse on duty, "Where are the Mason's?" She immediately said,

"Mrs. Mason is in surgery." John shifted his feet nervously impatient.

"The children are in emergency being treated Sir."

"I'm not Sir," he yelled I'm her son, and those are my children!"

"Excuse me S—, oh sorry."

"Your father went to the family waiting area with a priest, and your wife is in with the children."

"Take me to my wife and children now," he bellowed.

"Come with me S—, sorry she stammered." She led him through swinging double doors into a maze of curtained off partitions. He plaintively yelled,

"Lisa where are you?" He could hear children crying, it tore at his heart. "Here John," she stuck her head out so he could see her.

"Honey, it's not as bad as we imagined it might have been for the kids, and I don't know yet about mom." As John went in he saw Alex first; a nurse was cleaning up his cuts and abrasions.

"John, they think this may be all that's wrong with Alex. He goes to x-ray next to be sure." Lisa pulled the curtain back in the next section where a nurse and doctor were working on both Cecilia and Willie. They were both crying, their cuts were worse than Alex's.

"God Lisa, the bone," his voice broke.

"The bone is sticking out of Willie's arm," he said. John couldn't take it in all at once it was more than he thought he could bear.

"Calm down John" Lisa said.

"We can't be any help to them if we don't." He knew she was right but his emotions were ruling now. It ran through his mind how ludicrous it was of Lisa holding him together this time. 'Thank God' he thought.

Lisa went to comfort the twins, and John stayed with Alex.

"It's going to be all right son, dad will be here with you." He bent down and kissed his face and held his hand. Holding on he turned to Lisa and looked at Cecilia.

"Lisa, her leg—it isn't right is it?" She touched his arm and said "No it's broken but they will both be all right, they'll heal!" John felt as helpless as when Lisa was having the twins.

'At least the blood is cleaned up and that looks better,' he thought.

"Alex, I will be right back you can see me okay?"

A small voice bravely said "okay Daddy." John went around the other side of the gurney to kiss and help comfort both Cecilia, and Willie, they had them together but at opposite ends.

"I love you Ceci and Willie," his voice broke again.

"Stay with them Lisa, I'll be with Alex in x-ray. Whoever finds out about mom first will come find the other."

"Agreed" she said, as John followed Alex on the gurney to get his x-rays.

Willie and Cecilia continued to cry in pain.

"Can't you give them anything yet?" she asked the doctor. He finished adjusting the oxygen flow to Willie.

"Yes, we're starting an IV drip with pain medication now."

"Thanks," she said barely audible, "I need a chair." Lisa felt dizzy and faint all of a sudden.

"Here" said a nurse pushing a stool to her. 'Take a few deep breaths' she told herself, and the dizzy feeling will leave, she'd been holding her breath and was about to go out.

"All right now Mrs. Mason?"
"Yes, better thanks."

In the family waiting room, Father O'Brien kept Bill as occupied as possible talking. The surgery nurse came in with an update.
"Are you Bill Mason?"
"Yes."
"Your wife is in the middle of surgery and she is holding her own nicely. The doctor will be out and fill you in completely soon as he's done. It should be at least another half hour, and then she'll be in recovery for another hour."
"Thanks so much, please let me know when I can see her," Bill said. Father O'Brien put his arm around his shoulder. Bill clinched his jaw tight, still his eyes filled, Father O'Brien understood and felt an out pouring of compassion.
"Let's go to the chapel for a little while Bill, it will help."

The x-ray technician lowered the machine saying, "hold your breath Alex when I ask, so we can get some clear pictures please."
"Okay," he said. They took x-rays of his entire body, it took quite awhile. John reassured him saying, "You are the bravest man I've ever know Alex."
"Really Daddy?"
"Really son, I am so very proud of you! Without you there with gramma Marcy it would have been awful."
"Why?"
"You helped her Alex, you were the only man there with her to help, and you made Ceci and Willie feel better too. You're their big brother you know!"
"I was glad to help gramma Marcy Daddy I love her. Ceci and Willie needed me too because they cried very loud!"
"Yes, that's exactly what I mean."

The technician came in saying, "well young man I'd say you were very lucky. The only bone broken is in your nose and that will heal up fast."

Before long an attendant came to wheel Alex back to emergency for the doctor on duty to set and tape his nose. John was told they'd keep the children over night for observation.

"Can we arrange to have them in the same room please?"

"Yes, we can do that, no problem, I'll come back and let you know what room number it'll be, as soon as I find out."

John said "thanks that means a lot."

"No problem Mr. Mason, glad to do it," she said.

CHAPTER 25

"Excuse me," Lisa said to a nurse she passed, "where is the family waiting room?" The nurse directed her, and she joined Bill to wait while the twins were in surgery getting their bones set. Seeing him, their emotions that they were holding back opened up. He hugged her tight saying, "Lisa, it's going to be all right I love you honey you'll see. You are the daughter that mom and I always wanted. You must know by now, that you make our family complete. Tell me, how the children are doing?"

"Thank you Dad let's see, I just learned from the nurse that Alex has a broken nose. He also has some cuts, abrasions, and bruises. They've set and tapped his nose. The twins are in surgery to set their broken bones. Cecilia has a broken leg and Willie has a broken arm. Willie's is a bad break with the bone protruding but they will pin it and put it in some new type cast. Guess we'll find out later, but no concussions. They're going to keep them together in the same room over night for observation. John was able to arrange that for them thank God. He's with Alex now Dad, and will join us as soon as he can."

"By the way Dad, where is Father O'Brien?"

"He had to leave Lisa, but said he'd be back later tonight to talk to you and John. So far he is the only one that's seen Marcy. They let him in for a minute before surgery so he could give her communion, and the sacrament of healing. When she gets out of recovery we can go in one at a time, but she'll be heavily sedated!"

"You go in first Dad, then we'll take turns. I'm going to get us coffee, bet you could use some."

"Yes, I could—Lisa—thanks."

"Mom is in recovery Lisa, in fact you just missed the doctor. He said she should be fine after her recovery, but she sustained the most serious injuries."

"What happened, do you know Dad?"

"Yes, the police came earlier while you were with the children and read the report to me. A drunk driver ran the stop sign at the corner coming home. He hit the Suburban broad side, crushing Mom's side door. I believe we're blessed, it could have been much worse. The drunk driver died on impact!"

"What did they do in surgery, what did the doctor tell you?" Lisa asked.

"I'm sorry honey," he said "I'm so tired I can't think straight. They removed her gall bladder, cleaned all her deep cuts and closed her deepest wounds with staples. She must have bunches of them from the description. Her left leg was broken, and they set it. Both Cecilia and gramma will have casts on their legs! She also has a concussion, which worries the hell out of me. Even with her seat belt on, her head hit the side window hard. Far as I know that's it!"

"I'm so sorry Dad, that I asked mom to get the kids," tears welled in Lisa's eyes.

"Don't start that sweet one, I thought we had that covered, we are family and take our lumps together. Besides, I'll bet you Marcy will say she's glad it was her instead of you, so there! I'll go now and find out how the boys are doing. Is the doctor coming here when he's done with the kids surgery?"

"Yes, oh here's the doctor now Dad, stay to hear."

"Surgery went well, the twins are both in recovery and stable. Cecilia's leg was twisted when it broke, but it set well. She may need physical therapy after the cast is removed in about six to eight weeks. Willie will also be in his cast about the same length of time. The pin will remain in for now to secure and stabilize the bone. It was one of the worst I've seen. Any questions?—No, all right I'll see you in the morning, they should be able to go home tomorrow."

"Thanks so much good night doctor."

"Wow, what a day this has been. Dad, I completely forgot about your flu how are you feeling?" He looked sideways, and gave her a smile,

"I feel fine now, all this has cured me!" It wasn't really funny but they both laughed.

"I'm leaving now" Bill said, "to phone Amos and tell him the news, remember we promised."

"Yes I do, and give him my love," Lisa said. "I will Missy! See you later."

When John came into the waiting room Lisa began to tremble and felt cold. "Come here sweetheart," they stood there and held each other for a very long time drawing strength from each other.

"Can you believe this, Lisa?"

"Yes, but it is hard to take in and I know we're all tired let's sit down and rest.

Later we can all go up when they bring in the twins from recovery."

"Do you want to stay all night Lisa?" She nodded yes.

"That's what I thought," John said. A nurse came in and told them that Marcy was in ICU now.

"I'll go in first then," Bill said. When they went in and saw all the tubes they were upset. The nurse explained that the tubes and heart monitor were routine and precautionary.

After they saw Marcy, Lisa said "let's go up and check on the kids. Then maybe we can rest a while in the waiting room together."

Alex was fast asleep, "look" John said, "they're all sleeping, and as long as they sleep there's no pain."

"I know" Lisa said, "still I want to stay here in their room in case they wake up. You two go back to the waiting room, it's late nearly midnight, if Father O'Brien is coming he'll probably be there by now."

"Yes you're probably right Lisa, I hadn't even looked at the time. I understand why you want to stay here and I'll be up later too," John said. Father O'Brien was there when Bill and John came in. He said, "how is everyone doing, Marcy? The children?" After they told him what had taken place, he stopped by to bless and pray for the kids before he went home. That was how the new day began, at *Meade* hospital, they stayed the night together checking back and forth on each other, and on Marcy.

The doctor in charge of the children released them the next day. There were many instructions, to be followed, medications to be filled, and follow up appointments to be made; but John and Lisa took Alex, Cecilia, and Willie home!

They received lots of attention from everyone; Amos was first to come visit. "Hello you kid-lets, what's this I hear about all this stuff? Broke bones, cuts an all those gory things? Who's going to show me their cast first?" Amos had a huge bag in his hand filled with unknown things!

Alex spoke first, "me-me first, see Amos my nose got broke can you sign my nose please, and what's in the sack?"

"Yep, I'll sign your nose and as for what's in the sack you'll just have to wait till later! Hi Cecilia, how you feelin honey?"

"Better-Mos, she couldn't say the 'A' yet, will you sign my leg cast please?"

"I sure will Ceci, and girls are first!" Lisa had a box of color markers just for that purpose. Amos chose a red one and made a big heart, and signed love Amos.

"Lisa, give me a green one for Willie please."

"Here you go," she said.

"You sure are a brave boy Willie," he proceeded to sign the cast with a truck, sort of, and wrote heal fast love Amos.

"Okay Alex, big brave brother your turn, let's have the blue one Lisa." She handed it to him. Amos drew a badge and wrote brave inside it very gently, then signed it the same with love.

"How's that kids?"

"Thanks great," they all spoke at once.

"Now can we see what's in the sack?"

"Yes I guess it's time," Amos pulled out coloring books, sticker books with stickers and of course new crayons for each of them.

"Oh boy, thanks Amos come and see us again please."

"Ol Amos has to go to work now but I will come back and visit you, bye for now kids."

"Bye Amos" they said in trio!

"Thanks so much Amos, that will keep them busy," Lisa said.

"Say Missy, I've been meaning to talk to you about that nuisance of a Mulberry tree out yonder near the pasture gate. It makes an awful mess in the spring and summer with the berries. How about we have the crew cut it down for fire wood?"

"Amos, I love that tree, it's my favorite and it gives a lot of shade to the pasture. If it were up to me I'd say no, but I'll talk with John about it and have him get back to you."

"Okay Lisa, thanks I'd appreciate it."

Marcy was still in ICU. Bill was there this morning visiting her. John and Lisa planned to take turns between home and visits with her at the hospital. The phone rang and Lisa picked it up,

"Hello, yes Dad oh that's' great. I'm so happy she's awake. Is she in pain?"

"She says very little now, but earlier she was, they gave her a pain shot. She says to give you and the children her love and she'll see you and John later."

"Tell her I love her too, did you call the main barn?"

"Yes, honey John knows I phoned there first. Kiss the kids for me, I'll be home later."

"Okay Dad, thanks love you-bye."

The next day Marcy was moved into a regular hospital room for another week of recovery. She hated it but looked forward to their visits. Bill brought her home the following Monday morning. When Lisa walked over to visit taking her a bouquet of flowers she gave her a hug and kissed her. The first thing Marcy said was, "Lisa, I can't explain how thankful I am it was me in that Suburban with the kids and not you, I love you so much." They both had tears in their eyes. "It's great to have you safely home Mom. I talked to my folks, and they asked me to give you their love. They will be up to visit all of us when they can. They wanted to give us a chance to recover a little before they came."

"You tell them for me they're family and to come whenever they want," Marcy said. Bill agreed, and couldn't resist saying "see Lisa, I told you she'd say that!"

"Okay Dad, I'll mark that one down for you," smiling at them both.

It was a difficult time for the Mason's. They hired temporary help to work with the horses, allowing more time for family. Lisa's folks came for a few days and helped them before going home.

Weeks passed and finally they took the casts off. Alex first with his being taped, guess nose's heal faster. The doctor was amazed how fast their cuts and bruises healed. Cecilia said "Ouch it hurts" after the cast was off as the doctor fingered her leg to check the bone. "Sorry Cecilia" he said. "Looks like your leg will be good as new in a few months."

"Oh goodies," she said. Willie had to wait another week before he could do without his arm cast and then had to wear a sling for a while.

"Now Willie," the doctor said.

"I want you to do your exercises like we showed you—everyday. Will you do that?"

"Yes I promise," Willie said.

"Good kids you have there" he said to Lisa and John.

"Bill, I am so sick of all this I'm itching to get this cast off and move around more."

"I know you are Marcela but try to be patient, you know what the doctor said.

It takes time to heal injuries like yours."

Marcy made a face at him and said, "ahh shit, I know I should be happy to be alive, and I am but damn I want this over."

"Shit's a good word for it," Bill agreed.

"The whole mess of the accident was the shits and should never have happened. The poor kids too."

"Don't get me started on that one, and just when are you going to take me over there to see them?" Marcy said impatiently.

"In about a little minute, how's that sound," Bill said obligingly!

"Good" was all she said back.

By the time Marcy's cast was off and she was completely ambulatory spring had turned to summer and they all had cabin fever and itchy feet. Other than the scars they all bore both inside and out it appeared there would be no permanent damage or paralysis. For that they were all thankful to God. It felt like time to make arrangements for a late summer vacation for the whole Mason clan.

CHAPTER 26

*M*arcy was feeling much better, in fact she was thinking of doing something she rarely did, take off on her own and visit an old school chum. 'Gosh it would be so wonderful to see Patsy Cain again' she thought. On impulse she looked up her number and dialed it.

"Patsy?"

"Yes, who's calling?"

"It's me Marcy Mason, you know, Marcela Benson when we went to school together."

"Oh gosh Marcy, is it really you?"

"How are you, what's been going on?"

"Tons of things," Marcy said. "It's been so long, and we could never catch up in a few minutes on the phone. How about meeting me somewhere for lunch between *Meade* and Lexington, how does that sound?"

"Listen here Marcela Benson Mason, I've a better idea. You come spend a few days with me and we'll really catch up on old times; and all that's between, how bout it?"

"I don't know Patsy, what about your daughter isn't she still at home, I don't want to put her out of her room?"

"No you won't be. She moved to Chicago to live and work. Since we last spoke my husband Fred up and left, I'm divorced now. He found he liked the skirt of a younger woman and she said yes to him bless her! Perhaps I shouldn't make light of it, but things soured between us, so I'm foot loose as they say. We can eat, shop, talk, and go to shows as well as sleep in. How about that?"

"Yes, I'll do it. I'll come, it'll be fun, when do you want a house guest?"

"How about next Monday?" Marcy ran a myriad of thoughts and schedules through her head remembering the horse auction next week in *Meade* before saying, "Monday will be great,

If it's all right, I'll drive up and see you around noon?"

"Perfect, and it's warm so pack light clothes, maybe a sweater for the evenings, see you then, bye Marcy."

"Bye Patsy, and thanks I could use a good girl talk."

When Bill came in for lunch she could hardly wait to tell him.

"Honey guess what?"

"I can't imagine what Marcy, but I think I'm about to learn," he smiled at her.

"On impulse I phoned my old school friend Patsy Cain who lives in Lexington. She's invited me up next Monday through Wednesday for an old fashion girl talk, and shopping visit. What do you think? It's okay with you isn't it? You've got the horse auction next week and you'll be busy with that?" Bill's eyes were twinkling as he listened. He was used to these marathon spiels of talk from her.

"Oh and I almost forgot, the children, Alex will be visiting Jeb and Grace, and the twins will be in pre-school. That means Lisa won't need me to help her either!"

"Whoa…Good grief woman, that was a long story, of course I think it's a great idea. It'll do you both good to catch up."

"I have some news to share with you too. John and Lisa replaced the smashed up Suburban this morning."

"Great!" She said.

Bill continued, "they were tired of using the loaner van the insurance company loaned them." Marcy had that look, the one that told Bill she already knew what he was going to say.

"Yes, they bought another Suburban but instead of white this time Alex helped convince them they needed a bright blue one. At least that's what John said!"

"That's great I'm glad, the Suburban protected us from worse injuries.It gives me goose flesh thinking about how bad it could have been."

"Yes I agree on all counts, now what are we having for lunch lady? O'Conner the farrier's coming this afternoon. Warrior is being re-shod, and several others. Without a doubt that stud is unreal, the best we've ever had."

"I have to agree Bill, he is one pretty horse! I've seen every foal he's sired here and each one appears to have great conformation, and potential for the track, or as a pleasure horse."

"Next week at the auction, will tell the tale Marcy. We'll see how pretty the bidders think they are! Who knows, we may come home with a few new horses ourselves. John wants to buy a couple of ponies for the twins too."

"You usually do come home with more horses than you take!" Marcy smiled with a look of mock chagrin at him.

"Hi love" John said as he came in for lunch, "What are you up to?"

"The kids were playing and watching TV so I went on line to see what I could find in the way of information for our vacation in August. Remember, we're all going that last week in August and I know how they book ahead—everywhere so I was investigating. Mom and Dad said I could choose the place."

John pretended not to know what she was talking about and had his best perplexed look on.

"Don't tell me you forgot that,—you didn't John, you've always been the one to pick where we go." Lisa was wearing a pout on her pretty face.

"Silly woman, come here," Lisa grinned at him and snuggled happily into his arms. He held her face softly in his hands.

"Don't you know Lisa I'm putty in your hands, of course I didn't forget. Tell me, what did you find, where are we going?"

"Why don't you go on line right now and show me Lis." She logged on line and clicked the link that she'd saved into her favorites' file. Up came an ad for a *Berry Cove Resort* with lodge, and cottages on New York's Long Island. It had a gorgeous Atlantic Ocean view from the photos they were showing.

"Wow Lisa it looks impressive, what made you pick that one?"

"I'm not positive, but I remember reading or hearing, about how beautiful *Berry Cove* is.

It looks like a perfect place for all of us to relax and play. If you have no objections I'll phone and make reservations for both *Berry Cove* and our plane reservations this afternoon." John leaned down and pulled her hair up kissing her neck.

"John" she said, playfully, "what would the children think if they saw you doing that?" He pulled her up out of the chair and began kissing her face all over and whispered into her ear, "I think I'll eat you for lunch," he said with a roguish look.

"To answer your question, if you haven't forgotten what it was Lisa? I think the children would think their daddy loves their momma! I also think you should book us for that *Berry Cove* place."

"I will," she said and wished they were alone in the house and gave him the look that said so. She kissed him till he began to fondle her and then she quickly pulled away saying, "Sir you don't think I'm that kind of girl do you?"

"Actually I don't, at least not until I've eaten my lunch, and not until tonight! I've got to get back soon Lisa we've a busy afternoon."

"All right," she said and smiled, "I have your lunch ready in the frig, the kids and I have already eaten, so I'll just watch you eat. I'll pretend it's already late tonight with every bite you take."

"You are a little witch," he said, and winked at her.

With Alex, Cecilia and Willie taking their naps, she phoned and made their plane reservations. Then she nervously dialed the business number for *Berry Cove*.

"Hello, *Berry Cove Resort*, how can I help you?" Lisa hesitated, 'I know that voice' she thought nervously, 'it sounds like Nancy Panaé but how could that be?'

"Hello," she said. "I'd like to make reservations in August for our family." She was filled with nostalgia from long ago; but didn't have the nerve to ask who she was speaking with. Tears stung her eyes.

"When would you like to come?"

"Do you have any openings the last week in August, Friday the 24th, through Thursday the 30th?"

"Yes, but not in the main lodge, in the cottages how many will there be?"

Lisa was nervous. "There will be four adults, and three children."

"Each cottage sleeps at least four, and we have spare beds. We could add one," she said. Lisa cleared her throat and wiped her eyes.

"Yes, we'll need a double bed, and three twin beds in one, that would be perfect, I'd like two cottages that week please."

'It's done, I did it!' She noticed the address, 'it has to be near, or next door to my mother Lynne's home. Never could I forget my first mom,' deep yearning filled her heart. Lisa prayed asking for strength, remembering she would be given the grace to face anything. She whispered a silent thanks to God and blew her nose.

"It's time to clean house," she said to nobody. As she vacuumed she reminisced about old times. She also was thinking about John and their conversation about buying two ponies for the twins next week. She thought, 'it will be so much fun to take rides as a family.' She asked John not to sell Tuesday. She was very fond of her, and knew she'd be perfect for her to ride. 'I can see it all now, with Tag following after us, except when he runs ahead.' Lisa smiled wistfully at the picture in her mind.

She also thought of her trip to Georgia next week and decided to phone the folks.

"Hello Momma."

"Hi Lisa how are you, and how's the family?"

"All fine, I was just calling to firm up our drive down with Alex to visit you next week, is Monday still all right?"

"Sure is honey, and we're all looking forward to it, your daddy is ecstatic. He has big plans to show Alex all around the place, and let him learn more about the care of horses. After all this will be his home some day. "We are all settled into the big house now, it's so nice I love it. Sally has one of the large bedrooms, and we love having her live with us. You two will have fun catching up on each other's news. I'll let her tell you the details but she loves nursing school. Is John coming with you?"

"No, not this time he has to stay and work, this is one of the busiest times as you know. He would love to come too; it's killing him that I will be first to drive the new Suburban any distance. We just bought it this morning, the insurance company settled that part of our claim."

"Sure happy they did sweetheart, it's a good solid automobile. You sure do sound happy, do you have all those wrinkles ironed out of your life now?"

"I don't think you ever get all the wrinkles out Mom but it's true, I'm very happy, and yes most wrinkles are ironed. The accident was hard to go through but I believe it's made us stronger and closer as a family. That part of it is the only plus!"

"How's Marcy?" Grace wanted to know.

"Oh you know how mom Marcy is, always a trooper and she is feeling fit enough to go to Lexington to visit a friend next week."

"Well that is good news. Okay love, we'll see you and the children Monday when you get here. We'll have your beds all ready for you. Then the next day you and the twins can start back. We're so glad you have the new Suburban, did you say what color it is?"

"It's blue, bright blue thanks to that Alex of ours. He's a character!"

"We're all looking forward to your coming, bye for now."

"Bye Momma, give my love to Daddy."

On Long Island Berry Cove New York

From her front porch Lynne Elliot stood looking out over the ocean. It was evening, as she enjoyed the sunset with thoughts of Cassy on her mind. She sighed heavily, 'At least she is with my sweet Lee.' Stars were beginning to appear and she wistfully looked up wondering if they could see her. Sentimental me,' she thought.

"Oh hi Nancy, how was—your day? I didn't hear you coming."

"I hope I didn't startle you, you seemed lost in your thoughts."

"I was Nancy, I was thinking of Cassy and wondering what she'd think of our lodge and the cottages."

"I know she'd be thrilled for you and how you invested the insurance money after her death. Most of all she'd be happy to know I was living here next to you, helping you manage the business. How long has it been? It's been two years hasn't it, time goes swiftly. She'd be glad that my real estate business is flourishing. I miss her too, there have been many times I'd have loved to ask her advice about this or that."

"I know what you mean, I've wanted to ask her things too. I would have been absolutely lost without you Nan. You are loved as much as I love my Cassy." Nancy fell into the habit of calling her mom Lynne, it felt natural.

"Thanks and I love you too, this is home for me! Sure I'll always visit my family in Oregon when I can, but this place, the smell of the ocean I love it as much as you do. When Cassy spoke of it her last Christmas with you I knew I had to see this home of yours, to know this coast as she described it."

"Not to change the subject," Lynne said, "but who do you know of that has a larger collection of sea shells than we do!" They both laughed.

"Let's go fix us a bite to eat aren't you hungry too?"

"I could eat raw hamburger, right about now!"

"Well then come and help me peel the potatoes Nancy."

Berry Cove will be all that Cassy, now Lisa—remembered and more. In August the height of summer's beauty takes ones breath away. The flowers respond to the climate by growing larger and deeper in hue. Lynne and Nancy both loved to plant vegetable and flower gardens in the spring. It's an easy stroll to the surf and the view from *Berry Cove* is one of the finest along the eastern seaboard.

CHAPTER 27

Summer—July 1990
"There is nothing more powerful, nor more beautiful than true love in its fullness."

With Alex visiting her folks in Georgia, Cecilia, and Willie in summer pre-school *Mason Haven* was blissfully quiet. All the men were at the *Meade* horse auction selling the yearlings, foals, and buying new stock.

Lisa was unaware of her beauty as she walked with long feminine strides, easily swinging up onto the fence rail to sit and think. Sunlight filtered down on her causing her skin, and hair to shine like bronze. Light caught everything through the branches, adding much to the pristine beauty. She breathed deeply the fragrance of it all. The scent of grass permeated the humid air. This freshness filled her senses; the aroma pleased her greatly. In the pasture the mares dosed lazily as their foals romped and played about. It was 10:30 on this bright summer morning. Moments earlier on her way out, she grabbed an apple off the table, and let the screen door slam behind her. Marcy was visiting her friend Patsy in Lexington and would be gone a couple more days. Lisa took a leisurely walk enjoying the solitude. Instead of mucking stalls, or doing laundry she knuckled the small of her back with one hand, while holding the apple in the other. Fatigue washed away, as she approached the paddock to relax.

Musing to herself, 'Amos wanted to cut her tree down. He said it was a durn nuisance in the spring, and summer with all those dad burn berries fallin all over the place. Why, this huge Mulberry tree is my sanctuary! It's long boughs cast shadows like arms around me. They spread across the gate, and into the pasture beyond.' A smile crossed her face remembering what John said a few days ago, 'I'm putty in your hands Lisa! Wow, that gives a woman power…'

Peace washed over her with indefinable feelings, as she thought of her children, all three healthy now. Love surged deep in her heart kindled stronger with the thoughts of John along with a tingling sensation from last nights lovemaking. He brought color to her deep bronze cheeks and a yearning for his return later this evening. A smile of contented bliss crossed her full sensuous lips. No one made her feel like John. He aroused passion within her to heights she never knew existed. Just the fragrance of his pillow as she made the bed brought heat, yearning deep in her groin.

So much had changed and taken place since the day she arrived home from the hospital with the twins born some two plus years ago. That was the same day as Cassy's accident! Little Alex was four years old then and waiting for her with a flower clutched in his chubby hand. Now he says,

"I'm a big boy, I'm six," and holds up six fingers. Oh yes, she had learned a lot with more to come! Their lives together would blossom in ways that would bring sadness, but also peace, joy and fulfillment in deepening love. Theirs was a love that only comes once. A burning hot fire for all the seasons of their lives.

Lately, it seemed like peering through a telescope backward. The present expanding, as her feelings of love for this place this land and these people so filled her days. Immeasurable joy was the thought that came to mind. Lisa bit into the apple and let the juice run. Still, there were intense moments of inner turmoil. She wondered of her old life as Cassy, and always of her mother Lynne. 'Will I see her next month on our vacation to *Berry Cove*? Was that Nancy's voice on the phone when I made our reservations?'

The narrowing view of what once was receded deeper into her memory. It seemed now to shrink into an even smaller shaft down that imaginary telescope in her mind. Still this thought persisted, 'forget Cassy? Never!'

For now the farm was all hers. Later she'd leave to pick up the twins from pre-school. She was content sittin here under her favorite tree.

"Shoot" she said out loud, thinking 'I'm not going to let Amos talk John into cutting this Mulberry tree down. I don't give a darn how messy it is or how many berries it drops! I think if all my days were like today I could live right here under it.' Her beautiful face wore a determined look!

After finishing the apple, Lisa climbed down off the fence and walked into the barn to check on the latest litter of kittens. She wanted to make sure they had water and food. "Here momma kitty," she called. She was rewarded with a loud "me-oow" and her five kittens following her from behind a bale of hay mewing. "Hello momma and how are your children today?" Lisa smiled as the large tabby meowed again, and purred rolling over at her feet.

"Your babies are so cute," she told her. "Bet you don't miss Cookie, she is a pest for you isn't she." She thought 'well do you really expect an answer to that,' and laughed. Cookie, Marcy and Bill's Spaniel had a bad habit of chasing all the cats unlike Tag who never did.

Bill said "she has to chase the cats because she's little. Chasing them fills her with confidence, makes her feel like she's a big dog and important!"

'Now that's a silly excuse if ever I heard one,' and she laughed aloud again.

After petting the kittens and relaxing in the shade she took a soft rope halter and lead, to the paddock where Tuesday and her new filly were. 'How cute she is, and all legs, another pretty chestnut with flaxen mane and tail, she's fine boned like her momma.' They both nickered when they saw her; she wasn't hard to catch.

"Come here Sweet Pea," she slipped the halter on and snapped the lead to the ring and began gently coaxing her, leading her around.

"See little one, now that isn't so bad is it." Lisa patted and stroked her all over. It was a tradition at Mason's to train the foals and horses with gentleness, patience and love. They never broke horses they gentled them rather than using cruel brute force. Neither Bill nor John allowed a whip. 'It just isn't necessary' she'd hear them say. Amos was the biggest marshmallow of all. Once she came into the barn and heard him baby talking Warrior. That was when Lisa decided she really loved ol Amos. She didn't let him know she'd heard him either.

'Well' she thought, 'this is enough training for you today Sweet Pea' and Lisa let her go. Checking her watch it was nearly time to pick up Cecilia and Willie. 'If I leave soon I can stop and buy those riding helmets we decided to get for the kids.' There was just enough time to go play with Warrior for a minute in the last paddock down the row. She'd grown to love this huge stallion that was gentle and sweet by nature. Lisa climbed the fence calling him, "Here Warrior, here boy." He came trotting up to her, she slid onto his back and just wrapped her arms around his huge neck talking to him all the while. When she slid off he nestled her with his head. Then took off like he was in a hurry to get somewhere. 'What power and beauty that magnificent animal has, I'd never tell a soul this but this remarkable horse is strong like John.' Lisa smiled and thought of tonight. 'I really miss him whenever we're apart—hurry night!'

Checking her watch again she began running toward the Suburban to go get the kids with her heart full of love.

As Lisa drove the streets of *Meade* toward the *Tack and Bridle Shop* she pondered her conversation with Sally. The night she and the children arrived at the folks they had a long talk in her bedroom. 'She said she loved nursing and would graduate soon. She also asked an unusual amount of questions about Amos! That really has me puzzled,' Lisa thought—as she parked and went into the shop. After buying the helmets she turned to go and over heard the clerks talking.

Lisa clearly heard one say to the other,

"That customer you just helped, how much will you bet me that she's part black?"

"Not a penny" the other clerk answered.

"I think you're right, she does look part black. Seems like more and more of them are moving into *Meade*. My parents say they're taking over the whole state."

"Well," said the first clerk "they breed like rabbits I hear!" My folks say, "if they're part black they're all black…"

This was the first racial slur Lisa had experienced since Cassy's soul entered Lisa's body and it bit hard. 'Oh well,' she thought 'I suppose it's to be expected and I'll let it go this time. If I ever hear anyone say one word to or about my children I will scratch their eyes out!' Lisa never forgot what she heard but kept it to herself, 'somethings are best left unsaid. After all it's really their problem hate and ignorance will eventually eat a person up inside.'

That night when they came home from the auction there was a lot of excitement.

"Hello Lisa," both John and Bill yelled.

"How was your day?" she asked.

"Come and see," they said. Amos was talking a mile a minute to Cecilia and Willie who were trailing behind Lisa as she went into John's arms. He picked both kids up and kissed them.

"Daddy has work to do now, I have to unload these horses," he said to them.

"Lisa honey take care please, be sure that they don't get hurt."

"I'll be watching close John." There were three trucks with horse trailers, all big ones that transported six at a time. First they unloaded two perfectly matched coal black Shetland ponies. Both had a star and blaze on their foreheads.

"How perfect they are," Lisa said. Both Cecilia and Willie were jumping up and down with excitement.

"Who will ride them?" they both asked wanting to know. Grampa Bill said, "who would like to ride them?"

Cecilia said "ME!"

Willie said "ME TOO!"

"What do you think daddy John, should we let them ride around in a circle leading them?"

"Yes, if they will promise to always wear their helmets. How bout it Lis go get them please."

"We promise," they both spoke at once.

"Sure honey they're right here in the back of the Suburban." Lisa brought them back and showed them how the buckle snapped on.

"Okay Cecilia" grampa said, "let me lift you up."

"Now you Willie, how's that?"

"Super" he said, "wait till Alex sees the ponies, are they ours daddy?"

"Yes, they are a gift with responsibility."

"What's raponsbilty?" Cecilia asked.

"It means you will learn how to take care of them and feed them as you get older. It also means remembering to always wear those helmets that your momma bought you today."

"Is Alex coming home tomorrow?"

"Yes," Lisa said "he is, daddy will go get him early tomorrow."

"Oh boy I can't wait till he sees the ponies now we'll all have a pony huh" Willie said.

CHAPTER 28

With Alex back home, and Marcy home tomorrow the Masons began to make arrangements for their vacation to *Berry Cove*. The reservations were set with their airline tickets secured; all that remained were business arrangements. Amos would do the managing in their absence; together Amos, Bill and John would hire on extra men to help. Interviews would begin next week; they wanted men that were good with horses. Amos was an excellent judge of character, and so were John and Bill. Once years back they had a young groom they hired that Bill caught hitting a horse in the barn. When he ordered him to stop he said, "no—the horse is stubborn." It made Bill so angry Amos had to pull him off the young man. He was fired and charges were pressed against him so he wouldn't be hired again to work with horses in their county.

In the mean time Lisa was planning a horseback riding picnic at the lake on *Mason Haven* with Marcy, Bill and Amos. She let Marcy settle in her first day back then went over to see her and talk it over. "Hi Mom, how was your trip and visit with Patsy in Lexington?"

"It was fun, I had a good time but missed you all like crazy even more than I imagined."

"I'm so glad you could get away and have fun."

"I did a good deal of shopping for our vacation in August come and see," she said. Marcy had clothes laid out all over their bedroom.

"See my new sun dress do you like it?"

"Yes, I especially like the tropical colors."

"There is something here for all of us. I chose this dress especially for you."

"Thanks Mom I love it, do you think it's too low cut?" It was in a warm shade of ivory that would be perfect on Lisa.

"No, I think a woman needs to get her husbands attention on occasion! You know, let their eyes wander toward your neckline a bit!"

"I heard that. Watch it you two" Bill said as he left to go to work.

"Bye Honey, see you at lunch" Marcy hollered after him. They laughed and looked at the clothes she bought for the children. The twins sun suits were adorable. Alex had big boy bathing trunks, (in blue of course) and there were new beach towels for everyone.

"Thank you Mom for all these gifts. I'm really looking forward to this trip and hope everyone loves *Berry Cove*."

"Ya know what Lisa, Bill and I have never been to the beach. I bet we'll both love it. I'm excited about our going and so is Bill!"

"Tell me about the horse auction, what'd they buy?"

"Quite a few horses, it was real exciting, they unloaded the ponies for Cecilia and Willie first. Just wait till you see them they're a matched pair. They also bought a young year old stud that has a lot of promise for the future, not as handsome as Warrior but I'm prejudice."

"I think we all are when it comes to him what else did they buy?"

"Would you believe twelve new brood mares that are as light and sure footed on their feet as Tuesday is."

"That's saying a lot because she is the prettiest mare we have in my estimation."

"No argument from me she's my horse now. She's delivered her foal, an adorable chestnut filly. You can see her this Sunday that is if you and dad are game for a picnic at the lake with all of us, how bout it?"

"I can pull myself together by then," Marcy smiled at her "want me to fry the chicken?"

"Yes" Lisa said, "and I'll make the potato salad and chocolate cupcakes."

"All right it's all set but the fun. I won't ride out with you guys, because my leg is still a little stiff. I'll bring the food out in the pickup that way it'll be fresh from the refrigerator. Always hate to take a chance with warm potato salad anyhow."

That night after the children were in bed Sally phoned to share her good news.

"I made it Lisa I'm a nurse" and then she began to cry.

"Sally, what on earth is it, what's wrong?" She could hear her blowing her nose. "I'm sorry Lisa, it's just that I miss my mom so much tonight. It would have made her so happy to know that I graduated."

"Sorry—don't be! I understand, really I do. Did you tell the folks?"

"Not yet they aren't home from shopping yet but I will. They treat me just like a daughter and I love them so much. There is something else too, it's about Amos."

"What about Amos?"

"I know now that I love him Lisa, and she began to cry again."

"What in the world is wrong with that Sally? I think that's exciting. Amos is a very nice man."

"Yes, I know that but I don't think he cares for me—I mean not like I care for him."

"One thing for sure" Lisa said, "you'll never know if you don't ask."

"You mean just ask him?"

"That's exactly what I mean. Can you drive up here this coming Sunday?"

"I suppose—why?"

"We're having a family picnic and I'll see to it that Amos is home alone. He'll probably be in the barn. You drive up and just say what comes from your heart, okay? Trust me on this Sally I have a pretty good idea about how Amos is thinking these days."

"All right, what time do you think I should arrive?"

"Oh I'd say about noon would be perfect!"

"I'll give it a try and then wait around for you so I can tell you how it worked out. Oh Lisa, your folks are home gotta go and tell them the news. I love you, bye and thanks."

"Bye Sally and you're welcome, see you Sunday afternoon."

Lisa sat in the dark thinking about Sally and what she said. 'I sure hope I'm right about this.' She wondered, sighed and went to find John. He was with Tag sitting on the back porch enjoying the cool breeze.

"Hi honey, I need to ask you a question."

"Go ahead shoot."

"Uhh," she hesitated cleared her throat and then said,

"It's about Amos and Sally. There is this problem, Sally is in love with him."

"Oh," John said.

"What the heck does 'Oh' mean John?"

"It means I'm not sure if he's still involved with Clarese Lampson. I know he was for awhile. I'll find out for you and see if I can get a feel for how his thinking is about Sally, okay sweetheart?"

"That would be perfect John thanks so much. Sally's really hung up on him." John reached up and pulled Lisa by the hand to sit next to him. She'd been so intent on what she was talking about she stood the whole time. Lisa patted Tag's head, and John thought about Lisa's mouth. When one thought of a woman's mouth makes a man crazy for her he's in love.

"Lisa!"

"Yes John."

"Let's go to bed." Lisa smiled in the dark.

In Georgia, at *Windsor Farm* Jeb and Grace just heard the good news from Sally. They were very proud, and happy for her.

"Congratulations Sally, we're so very proud of you, just think an education is something nobody can take away from you."

Jeb and Grace were extremely happy for her; both hugged her tight.

"Thank you both for all your love and support. It means a whole bunch to me. I so cherish being part of your family and living here with you. It's true about nursing, now that I am a L.V.N. I can probably find work just about anywhere."

"Absolutely, and you will always have a home here Sally for as long as you want. When Lisa married it sure filled our hearts having you near."

"Good night to you both and have sweet dreams."

"Same to you Sally" Grace said giving her another hug.

Sally sat looking at herself critically in the mirror. She frowned at herself thinking, 'what I am is—ugly!' She continued brushing her black hair thinking 'my nose is too big, I'm too fat, but oh how I wish

I was pretty. If I was then maybe Amos could learn to care about me maybe even love me.'

As many of us are Sally was also a mixture of ethnic heritage. Just as Lisa has a varied rich heritage of African American, American Indian, Caucasian, and God knew what else. That is a fact, but Sally was pretty, it was a shame she didn't know it. Her dark brown eyes were huge and shiny, her lips full but not overly so. Her hair was curled tight but not frizzy or dull. It shined like a raven's back. When she smiled she could light up any room. She didn't know it though any more than Lisa did before she was married! The difference now was, Lisa was loved and that was her security, which made her feel beautiful without any vanity. Instead it humbled her soul to be so cherished. Being loved is a need so basic that it is near impossible to thrive without it. During the days preceding Sally's planned trip to see Amos she did all she could to prepare herself. 'What's the worst thing that could happen' she'd reason; 'if he says he's sorry that he could never love me. If that's how it is, I'll just have to face it and fill my life with other things like work, ugh' she thought! Still, I love people and now I can support myself.' Lisa phoned Sally Saturday afternoon saying, "I can tell you this much Sally Amos is not seeing anyone now John asked him."

"Thanks Lisa, that's good news," she said.

"When you get here be sure to tell Amos that you're the delivery that he is waiting for, and drive safely."

"I will Lisa, and thanks so much." It was with all this in mind that she left Saturday night to learn her fate, at least that's how Sally saw it.

At *Mason Haven* all was ready for the picnic. Years ago when John was a boy Bill took an old picnic table with attached benches out near the lake in his pickup. Lisa arranged with dad Bill to have Amos eat his picnic at or near the barn area instead of going with them as originally planned. He told Amos:

"A delivery is coming that can't be missed, I need you to be here." That was all it took from his boss and oldest friend. Amos didn't even question him! Lisa and Marcy saw to it that he had more than enough to eat and a cooler of beer! While the rest of the family dined at the lake and had lots of fun Amos waited.

Sally looked at her watch it was 12:20 PM when she turned into *Mason Haven*. Whew, she breathed deeply inching up her courage. 'Just say what's in your heart,' she repeated to herself. She pulled her old beat up Plymouth to a stop under the shade of the disputed Mulberry tree. 'Wonder where he is, he is no where in sight.' Sally got out and slammed the door.

'What the hell was that?' Amos wondered, he was sprawled on a bale of hay taking a snooze after eating his lunch. 'Must be the delivery Bill mentioned,' he thought. Before he was on his feet Sally entered the barn and called,

"Amos, are you in here?"

'That sounded like Sally's voice, couldn't be' he thought.

"Yes, over here, is that you Sally?"

"Sure is, I want to talk to you for a minute please."

'What in the world could that pretty lady possibly want to talk to me about' he wondered.

"Sure, anything did you drive all this way to talk to me?"

Amos was astonished and puzzled. Sally was nervous, her face flushed!

"I did, and I have aah, I am the delivery." Now he—was puzzled.

"What kind of delivery?" he asked.

'Gosh she's pretty, and she looks like she has a lot on her mind too.'

"Nothing much Amos," Sally was looking at her feet as if there was a snake on them.

"I ah, I came to say that I love you Amos." Tears immediately welled up in her big eyes and threatened to spill. Amos stood looking at her with his mouth open not comprehending her words.

"Sally would you—please say that again? I'm not sure I heard you right."

She steeled herself and looked him straight in the eyes.

"Amos, I said I love you!"

Several seconds passed before he read it all in her eyes. With an expression of concern and tenderness he reached for her. 'My God, I'm shaking inside,' he thought. 'I really love this woman and was too stupid to realize it, damn' he thought to himself. 'What next,' as he took her in his arms and hugged her close.

"Sally," he said with a cracked voice. Without thinking she reached up and kissed him softly, then with her arms around his neck deeper. To her amazement Amos responded quickly. 'This must be what heaven is like' he thought, then he didn't think anymore he felt with his heart. His body followed! 'My whole being aches for her, an ache like I've never known.' His tongue probed the depths of her mouth, as his groin wanted more. Sally broke their kiss, and reached up doing something he'd never known. She traced his face with her finger and across his eyes with a look of such pure love. Amos picked her up and kissed her again with more passion than Sally had ever known. He caressed her body moving over her. 'I love her, I love her' over and over he thought as his hands wouldn't, couldn't stop his respectful and admiring feel of appreciating the whole of her as she moaned her pleasure. 'Say it to her you damn fool,' he thought. The words were stuck in his throat. Then…Finally!

"I love you Sally Jones, I love you, and I didn't even know it!" A look of complete astonishment filled his rugged tanned face. Sally just looked back at him no less surprised than he did. Joy was beginning to creep into the heat of her passion and heart. Out of the blue he said,

"Will you marry me?" Amos asked the question with such emphases on the word 'me' that Sally slowly smiled.

"YES" she answered and began kissing him lightly all over his face and neck.

"Whoa lady" he said, "My heart won't take much more of this right now." Amos wore a huge grin!

CHAPTER 29

On the lake at *Mason Haven* the afternoon sun was dropping its rays in such splendor. Jewels popping off the ripples of water shined like diamonds. They sat enjoying their last hour in contentment. The three children ran around like all youngsters do. Alex was giggling and chasing both Cecilia and Willie with a stick that had a bug on the end of it.

"Kids, slow down" John warned "so nobody falls and gets hurt."

Then Lisa broke the silence of the adults.

"I was hoping that by now we'd see a pickup drive out here with Amos and Sally in it." John put his arm around her and squeezed her waist.

"You are a natural born romantic aren't you!"

"Well me too," Marcy said and shaded her eyes peering down the road toward home. Within five minutes or less she exclaimed, "yes—oh my they're coming I see dust flyin and it's a truck coming!"

Amos parked the truck crooked, and they walked over to them wearing the silliest grins. That was of course when they all knew the answer to their question. Bill and Marcy just beamed smiles.

"Guess what," Amos said.

"What" said John and Lisa together.

"We're getting hitched" answered Amos.

"When" asked Marcy?

"We don't know," they both said.

"Guess we're just getting used to the idea that we love each other," Amos said. Lisa went over to Sally and hugged her tight kissing her cheek. Marcy walked to the pickup and came back with a surprise.

"I'm always prepared for a celebration," she said. "Champagne anyone?" While the kids continued to run around and pet their ponies paying no attention to them the adults all said "Yes," as Marcy and Lisa began filling and passing the plastic champagne glasses that Marcy had brought along just for this purpose.

"A toast to the future Mr. and Mrs. Amos Hardy" Bill said. They all lifted their glasses as if made of the finest crystal.

"May your troubles be few your joy complete and may your love last forever!"

"Here-here" they cheered each in turn wishing them their personal congratulations.

"I hate to be the one to break up our happy family gathering but we have a ride ahead and horses to feed" Bill said.

"Come on children" Lisa called. Marcy suggested she take the children home with her in the truck and they lead their ponies home. A good idea John and Lisa agreed.

"Let us hear when you set the date you two" John said.

Amos looked at Sally's bright smile and said, "if it's alright with my lady let's make it as soon after your vacation to New York as possible. You'll be back around the first of September right?"

"Yes," they said.

"Sally how about the second weekend of September?" Everyone quieted down and waited for her to answer.

"Sounds perfect to me, and Lisa will you be my matron of honor?"

"Yes" she said, "I would be honored and thank you Sally."

Amos looked over at John and smiled at him. He said "yes Amos I would be honored."

"Thanks Johnny there's nobody I'd rather have than you."

"We're both so happy for you…"

That night when Alex, Cecilia, and Willie were bathed and tucked in bed asleep, both Lisa and John listened as Sally, and Amos phoned Jeb, and Grace to share the happy news with them.

"Hello Grace, would you have Jeb get on the other phone please."

"Hi it's me, and Amos too we're sorry for calling late but we wanted to share our news. Today we became engaged!"

"Wow, congratulations to you both. That's super good news," Grace said.

"I bet you'll be wearing your best and prettiest smile when you come home" Jeb said.

"I'll be home tomorrow night sometime, and don't worry I'll drive safely."

"Okay you two kids, thanks for sharing with us, let us know when you set the date."

"Oh sorry, we've already set the date, it's to be the second weekend in September. That way there will be time to plan everything ahead. They'll all be home from their vacation in New York with time to prepare too. The reception will be here on the lawns of *Mason Haven*. Lisa, and John have agreed to stand up with us as matron of honor and best man."

"Not surprised about that," both Grace, and Jeb agreed. Congratulations again, and have a good night you two, see you tomorrow night Sally. Bye."

"Bye for now," Sally and Amos said.

The lover's went for a walk somewhere on Mason land.

John commented to Lisa, "if they're anything like we were they'll walk a long way."

"Yes" Lisa said smiling, "they will and it will be morning when Sally goes to bed—I bet. "No bets Lisa," John said smiling too, "because we both know the answer to that!"

Time drew near for their departure with all plans and arrangements made. It seemed as if Amos wore a perpetual smile and nearly burned up the phone lines between *Mason Haven* and *Windsor Stock Farm*. Of course Sally probably did her share of phoning too! They decided to hold their wedding in the same parish church where John and Lisa were married.

They said, "it worked out so well for you kids we thought it might bring us our own measure of happiness."

"We think so too," both Lisa and John agreed.

"In fact with the exception of our occasional disagreements we get along very well," John said. There was love and peace in their home, the abiding kind that helps children thrive.

The night before they were to leave all was in readiness. Amos was ready to drive them to the airport in Lexington. The alarm was set for 5:00 AM. When they sounded Lisa pushed the button, and said:

"All right kids, time to get up. everyone, you too John," she said with a smile.

"Yes I know you're sleepy," she said to the kids "but you can sleep in the Suburban and then guess what?"

"What" naturally followed by all three?

"Breakfast on the airplane all of us together, won't that be fun!"

The Mason's were on their way for their first all together family vacation. Marcy and Bill seemed as excited as the children.

Amos drove home from Lexington airport smiling. Sally was on her way to Mason's to bring some of her belongings!

Alex was looking out the window of the plane as they were about to land at LaGuardia International when all excited he said:

"Look Momma and Daddy, is that the Statue Of Liberty?"

"Yes Alex it is" Lisa said, "let's move Cecilia and Willie over so they can see it too."

"Hurry before it goes away" he said.

"Look Ceci, do you see it Willie?" Alex said excitedly.

"No, don't see it," said Willie. "See what?" asked Ceci.

"Don't worry Alex," John said, "we'll all be taking a trip on a boat to see the Statue Of Liberty later we'll be here a whole week."

"Oh good" he said. "I want to tell my new school class all about the statue, for show and tell."

Just then the 'Fasten Your Seat Belt' light came on, and everyone returned to their seats to buckle up for landing.

"John, shouldn't you wake mom and dad? They've been napping."

"If they don't wake on their own let's leave them to relax through landing Lisa. Their belts are fastened and there's plenty of time for them to wake after we land."

"Alright John good idea."

"I could tell they were extra tired this morning."

By the time they were at the Rent-A-Car area it was around eleven o'clock.

"What kind of car are you going to rent dad?" John wanted to know.

"Oh I don't know, what kind would you like Marcy?"

"Could we try a Firebird, or a Camero?"

"Sure, which one?" Marcy screwed her face into a thoughtful frown thinking.

"I'd rather have a Camero if one's available, if not a Firebird."

"They say they have a red and a yellow Camero, which one would you like?" He asked.

"You pick the color," she said.

"Good grief woman, okay the red one!" For some reason that tickled Marcy and she came down with a fit of giggles over Bill's reaction and choice of color. "A red Camero" she said laughing. Lisa laughed too picturing them driving along in it. John requested a Suburban if available; they had three in different colors. When John heard blue he took it, which made Alex ecstatic!

The drive to *Berry Cove* was full of excitement as the children saw one new sight after another. They were never more excited; Lisa and John smiled to hear them so full of wonder. Lisa wondered how patient they'd feel after a week of fielding all these questions! Meanwhile Bill led the way, and they followed as Marcy read the map to Bill. It wasn't a long drive from the airport but one they'd never made before. New York can be tricky to drive in especially for new comers.

Lisa pulled the brochure out of her purse and looked at it. The cottages were in the traditional cape cod style and looked inviting to her. Twinges of remembrance danced in the back of her mind, along with anticipation and excitement. 'Calm down she told herself, all will be fine.'

"I'm hungry," the children said plaintively in triplicate.

"Actually I am too John, what do you think?" He signaled to Bill and they picked a place for lunch before continuing. It ended up that they ate there quite a few times. They chose *Cap's Table,* which had delicious seafood and they served salt-water taffy to everyone at the end of their meals. The children loved it there was an aquarium with sea creatures and fish all along one wall. It was close to the resort in *Berry Cove*!

The view of the Atlantic Ocean as they climbed a hill outside *Berry Cove* was eye dazzling on this summers day. Gulls skimmed the surface of rough white capped waves as they ate their fill of fish. Sailboats caught the wind with their multicolored sails and billowed full as they cut through the surface. John hit the window buttons so they could inhale their first whiff of the ocean's unique fresh fragrance.

"I sure hope Dad and Mom will enjoy this vacation with us," Lisa said to John.

"Quit frettin honey, I'm sure they will it's all new to them and they've always seemed to enjoy being with us. You worry too much. Look kids we're here, this is *Berry Cove*. Lisa, I'll take care of getting the keys, just relax and enjoy the sights."

"Alright we'll get out and stretch our legs, how about it kids? Lets go talk with Gramma and see if she'll go take a look at the beach with us." Lisa helped the twins out of their car seats and Alex, undid his seat belt.

"Mom, want to walk on the beach and look around while Bill, and John get our keys for the cottages?"

"Can't wait I'm coming" she said and they all took a walk down to the water's edge.

"Look at those little birds" Alex said, "what are they Momma?"

"I think they're sandpipers," she said.

"See their long legs they run back and forth with the water and catch sand-crabs for food."

"Momma, what's a sand-crab," Cecilia asked?

"Here I'll show you." The next time the ripples receded from a wave Lisa quickly dug down and scooped up several wiggling sand crabs.

"See! Here Willie and Cecilia hold out your hands they won't bite. Here's another Alex hold it."

"It tickles my hand" he said.

"Yes, they tickle me too," Cecilia and Willie said.

"Hey," John and Bill called to them, "come on let's get settled in our rooms. Plenty of time for the beach later."

"Coming," they all hollered.

"What's—s-e-t-t-l-e-d" Willie asked?

"Come on and we'll show you, let's help Daddy and Grampa unload the Suburban and car." The rooms were large and comfortable with a small kitchen in each so they could eat snacks, have small meals or pack lunches to take to the beach.

"What's wrong Willie and Cecilia?" Lisa asked. They were both rubbing their eyes. "Are you sleepy?"

"No, but my eyes hurt" they said.

"OOP's hurry come into the bathroom both of you, Alex don't rub your eyes. Come on let's wash off the sand. I forgot you kids had sand on your fingers."

"Better?"

"Much," they agreed.

"Now lets go carry a few of your toys in from the car." When they finished moving in for the week they were tired. Lisa put the twins down to nap. Alex wanted to look for sand crabs, so with Lisa watching they walked the oceans' edge.

"Hey kids, we're going to take a nap too" Bill and Marcy said to Lisa. "We'll see you at supper time around 6:00 o'clock."

After checking on the twins who were fast asleep, John walked down to be with Lisa and Alex for a few minutes then returned to be with the twins. 'I could easily come to like this way of relaxing, it's great to be able to see the ocean from the window,' he thought.

CHAPTER 30

Lisa woke early. The cottage was quiet except for the even breathing of John and the children. Love filled her being, and crossed her face as she looked at them asleep. Her inward smile faded as her thoughts drifted towards Lynne, and Nancy. 'I haven't even caught a glimpse of them yet!' It was easier for her to simply call them by their names re-familiarizing her-self with the idea of seeing them.

In a cozy home near by, there was lively early morning chatter. Lynne and Nancy were enjoying the view, and their regular time of having morning coffee together.

"What's on your agenda today Nancy?"

"Oh, I have a huge two story home to show in South Hampton this afternoon. If it sells the commission will be generous and welcome!"

"Good luck," Lynne said encouragingly.

"Thanks, other than that I'll be home doing book work for the resort. It's time to pay those pesky bills again!" Lynne sighed. "Time rushes past me," she said.

"Seems I just balanced the bank statement for last month, now it's time to pay bills again!"

"I know it" Nan said. "Life has its way of speeding past us. I think I'll go on Lynne and get started. I hope you have a good day, see you tonight?"

"Yes, I'll be home, I'm re-doing my old photo albums and I'm reading a good book too."

"Alright then, bye for now" Nancy said as she left.

Lisa quietly dressed and slipped out the door to go for a walk. She left a note to John saying *'Don't worry, I'm walking I'll be back soon—Love You'* The ocean view was muted with moving eddies of fog as she looked out toward the horizon. 'It's just chilly enough I'm glad for my sweat shirt,' she thought. 'What a gorgeous view even in the shroud of moving fog!'

Lynne opened her front door to look at her flowers as Lisa came near.

"Good morning, out for a walk aye" Lynne said greeting her.

"Yes, hello good morning to you I'm Lisa Mason" she said.

"Well now, I'm happy to meet you I'm Lynne Elliot. Are you staying in one of my cottages?"

"Yes, my family and I arrived yesterday in the Suburban and red car. It's beautiful here, I love the freshness of the ocean air."

"Oh yes I do too. This is my home and I wouldn't trade it for anywhere else on earth. Say, how about a quick cup of coffee? I just made a fresh pot."

"That would be nice" she said as she whispered a silent word of prayer for strength. 'She looks wonderful and healthy, thanks God for keeping her safe.'

"Here, let's sit on the porch by the window, the fog will lift momentarily. Look! The sun is trying to burn through all ready!"

"You're right it's going to be a lovely day." Lisa sat by the open front door with a clear view of both the sea and the room within.

"I saw the children yesterday, they're yours?"

"Yes they are, and are they ever excited to be here!"

"They are adorable, you have a lovely family Lisa."

"Thanks" she said, "and lively too. They never seem to run out of questions."

Lynne commented, "that's a very good sign in children-curiosity!"

"Yes it is" Lisa said, "but tiring sometimes too."

Lisa moved, turning her head slightly and saw a photo of Cassy inside on a shelf. It hit with unexpected force as if the bottom of her stomach dropped.

'Oh my God, it's me…it's not me!' Inner turmoil surged and took over her mind. All the old memories merged in that instant. It was like a closet with boxes packed too high on the shelf, which teeter and fall. Memories fell on top of her head crashing and breaking her emotions, cutting them in a million pieces. 'I can't swallow can't breathe.' Spontaneously Lisa reacted coughing hard, then again swallowing followed as she caught her breath.

"My dear, are you all right?" Concern obvious on Lynne's face.

"Can I get you a glass of water?"

"Yes please," Lisa said barely audible. 'Breathe calmly she reminded herself.'

"Oh thanks, I must have swallowed the wrong way."

"You're welcome, are you sure you're all right?"

"Yes, I'll be fine in a minute." Lisa forced a smile as a flood of memory flashed through her mind again. 'I gave her that photo and frame on our last Christmas together. It's in the exact same place she put it after opening it. My chest feels like it's going to explode my heart is pounding as if it will burst. Please…God, give me some help or I'm going to loose it.'

"What are the names of your children," Lynne asked?

"What" Lisa said? "I'm sorry I didn't hear your question. The trip has left me more tired than I expected."

"Oh" Lynne said, "this salt air will let you sleep soundly tonight you'll see. I was asking the names of your children?" Lisa smiled at her answering,

"Alex is the oldest he's six, and the twins Cecilia and Willie are two and a half years. Speaking of them they'll be awake and hungry by now. I must be getting back. I thank you very much for the visit and coffee."

"You're welcome Lisa, come back please I've enjoyed our visit. You are welcome anytime. If I can be of any help just let me know I will be happy to. If I'm not home my assistant Nancy Panaé will help you up at the Lodge."

"Thanks," Lisa said as she hurried away. Soon as her head turned away the tears fell. 'Damn my nose is running too.' She wiped her face dry as she could with the full length of her shirtsleeve. 'Well dummy what did you expect. Nobody forced you to come here! What a surreal experience.' She stood in front of the cottage door thinking about it a moment and allowed time to compose herself. Peace came to her, she was flooded with it a peace that washes the soul in knowing you've come full circle. All is well! She took a deep breath then and opened the door to…Lisa's world and love.

Her emotions were like the door, fully open ready for anything with God's help. She stepped into the cottage to pandemonium.

"Hi honey," John said. He grinned and asked, "have a good walk?"

"Yes sweetheart" and went into his arms for a warm morning hug. "Come here you little muffins and give your momma a hug," she said to them. Lisa felt the fullness of love swell like the lump that was in her throat as they began their full day of plans.

"Let's go have pancakes with Gramma and Grampa," John said.

They heard a very cheerful and loud yes in triplicate from the children just as Marcy and Bill knocked on the door.
"Hello, anyone home in here, anyone hungry?"

On their return from the boat trip to Ellis Island and the Statue of Liberty the children were fast asleep in the back.
"I love you Mrs. Mason," John said. "How about a walk on the beach tonight if Mom and Dad will stay with the kids, is it a date?"
Lisa smiled up at his handsome face that she adored and said "it's a date, good lookin!" John simply grinned both inward and outward!

"Mom, Dad thanks so much," Lisa whispered as they grabbed up a blanket to take along with them.
"There is NO way we would have any time alone with these three even with them asleep!"
"Yes, we sort of knew that," they said quietly so as not to wake them. "Enjoy your walk and don't hurry children" they said.
"Thanks again," John whispered! "You're welcome," they answered.

They held hands and walked the shoreline. The evening was unusually balmy for a late August evening. Not even a hint of a cold breeze. Not a word was spoken, allowing their hearts to commune. They passed a copse of low slung junipers, their fragrance blended, adding to the scent of the ocean air. He stopped, looked at her face in the pale twilight bent and kissed her closed eyelids. First one, then the other he could feel her lashes with his tongue. Standing on her toes she reached his ears resting her lips there and lingered tasting the saltiness of his skin. The savor, the scent of him, her skin aroused and tantalized him till they were side by side on the blanket. Stars their witness of passion as they lifted each other in communion of their bodies. He memorizing her form of soft curves, and kissing her inner thighs. Then her sweet wetness, the soft hair and her rose of skin between which hungered for him. His maleness his strength filling her deeply plunging hard in the heat of their ancient dance of love. When at last love's passion was satisfied they looked at the night sky, the stars and felt whole. In each other's arms they lay for a long long while. They listened to the tide, to the beating of their hearts matching the rhythm of life.

The Mason clan enjoyed their days together in the waning summer sun. There were walks alone and together. Side trips galore, and one day when Lisa was walking while John and the children slept she nearly ran into Nancy. They both said,
"Excuse me," Lisa recognized her dear familiar face and voice.
"Say aren't you the lady I spoke with to make our families reservations? I'm Lisa Mason."
"Hello Lisa, yes I am the one! I'm Nancy Panaé, glad to meet you. I hope that you are enjoying your vacation."
"Thank you Nancy we are, this is a heavenly place to visit and I understand from Lynne Elliot that it is a year round haven for you both. Have you lived here long?"
"Oh let's see, about two years give or take a week or so I'd say." Nancy smiled and said, "you know I didn't plan to stay here just to visit my friend and perhaps lend her a hand after the loss of her daughter. I just fell in love and stayed, been here ever since. I have a few family members left in Oregon; it's pretty there but nothing like this. Why *Berry Cove* surely must be God's place!"

One of the days while there, Marcy and Lisa converged on the men.
"Hey, how about we shop, and you play—with the children on the beach!?"
"Okay," they both dutifully agreed. Marcy and Lisa had a great time shopping for everyone. They ate lunch out, and both had their hair done. It was an all around perfect girls day. Bill, John, and the

kids enjoyed their day of play on the beach. That evening they thanked Mrs. Elliot for her kindness, and prepared to leave *Berry Cove*. They packed everything up for the return trip home. The next morning, their flight from New York to Kentucky was safe and uneventful.

As they turned into the driveway Alex said, "that was fun, but there's no place like home huh Momma?"

"That's for sure Alex we're all happy to be home again," Lisa said. Cecilia, and Willie were sound asleep as they unloaded the Suburban. Bill gave Amos an affectionate slap on the back and asked, "how have things been while we were gone?" Amos smiled that slow smile of his and said, "Smooth boss, real smooth!"

"We all owe you a debt of thanks Amos," John said. He shrugged his broad shoulders and said,

"Heck, no thanks needed my pleasure, we're a family here at Mason's."

"Yes we sure are," Marcy said to him. "Are you about ready for that wedding?"

"About as ready as I'll get I suppose," Amos drawled.

Marcy and Lisa brought home many lovely gifts for Sally's trousseau little things she'd never splurge on for herself. Sally told Lisa before they left it would be fine with her to go ahead and choose her dress for the wedding and reception without her but please choose a pink one. She found a soft pink silk that skimmed her body like a loose glove, then flared out at the hem. The whole effect was one of femininity. Sally also told her that she was going to ask her father Jeb to give her away. Lisa knew it would thrill him to do so and she looked forward to the special day. As for the men they would rent their suits! It was a small wedding of about fifty close friends and family. They decided to cater the luncheon on the lawn of *Mason Haven*. It had worked out so well for Grace, Marcy, and now Lisa not to have to cook! They could enjoy wedding and reception without a care or worry.

The junior and senior Mason's gave the newlyweds a honeymoon gift to where else—*Berry Cove Resort*! It appeared that everyone enjoyed themselves so much that *Berry Cove* would be a favorite vacation spot again and again! Grace and Jeb were more practical; they gave them a clock and a lovely bedroom set, which they chose together. It seems Amos had always just slept on his fold out sofa. Lisa joked with both mom's that she figured that their home will under go a lot of major change under the guiding hands of Miss Sally herself—soon to be Mrs. Sally! Lisa was quite right about that.

Besides Lisa's experience at *Berry Cove,* she didn't know that while there Lynne Elliot was also having an experience. It bordered on the paranormal. Lynne didn't understand it, but felt something prickly at the base of her mind fundamental and primal when they were together. Intuitively she sensed that there was a tie between Cassy, and Lisa yet it made no sense. No matter how hard she tried to persuade herself otherwise the thought persisted. Each time she saw Lisa and the children on the beach it stirred her emotions of Cassy deep within. Lynne recognized it as a deep truth on some level. Once while Lisa walked the shore with the children she saw Cassy walking beside her…bright and clear. So profound was this viewing that she rubbed her eyes and looked again. She saw Cassy with them! That night Lynne couldn't sleep. She lay awake and relived it repeatedly. 'What is real?' She wondered and questioned the fundamental rules about life. 'Where does the reality of life leave off, and where does the veil of the unknown begin? Why is the mist over this strange dimension lifting now?'

After the Mason's left *Berry Cove* for Kentucky it played over in her mind. She argued, 'this cannot be so, it defies logic.' Lynne didn't discuss these thoughts with Nancy, and perhaps never would. This was something very special, cherished and private. She was a deeply spiritual person so she held this mystical gift close in her heart. It replayed in her mind, and she willed it to do so. Her heart pounded with it and she had an adrenaline rush so strong it frightened her.

'What to do—nothing?' At night she lay awake pondering all this. 'The children themselves draw me. It's as if I know them, and their mother. Yes—like I've always known them, or knew them before! This I know, when they were here I felt Cassy's presence strong all around me and with them. After they arrived when I first spoke with Lisa I felt it. When I got her coffee, and then the glass of water it felt like I was getting it for Cassy…They look nothing alike, not even remotely. The closeness must be spiritual. Truth then…Logic has nothing to do with it!'

If it's possible to walk into the mist of another person's dream then that's just what Lynne and Lisa did…it simply happened! The second night after returning home Lisa dreamed of her mother Lynne, *Berry Cove,* and Cassy. At the same time Lynne saw herself entering Lisa's dream. Cassy and Lisa were together, clear bright and lucid as one person. When they woke, they both knew they'd shared this awareness of what was, and what is beyond. Each knew at the same moment this truth. Lynne knew she would see Lisa and her children again some day. Were Lisa's children her grandchildren? It no longer mattered that she didn't understand! To know that her daughter was alive thrilled her.

Early that morning Lynne woke abruptly. She sat engulfed in the moment with her dream. It was just before dawn. She got up dressed, and put on her coat against the fog going out to cherish this blessed wonder. 'Thank you God' she thought prayerfully, 'thanks so much.'

The sea was calm. It was low tide only a gentle breeze stirred the air. Suddenly she felt she wasn't alone. She turned, looked around but saw no one. There—it came again quite real. Her right hand felt warm and held by another. This time she turned abruptly to her right and saw the profile of Lee, her Lee holding her hand. With her heart in her throat she opened her mouth to say—then nothing. She felt him squeeze her hand in his, as his image faded away.

Lynne wrapped her arms around herself in a hug of thanksgiving. "I am not alone, not at all," she said. Then went home to have coffee and ponder all of this.

'Oh for goodness sake' she thought I left the door open. 'Silly me.' After pulling her coat off she poured water into the pot and began the morning ritual of making coffee. Lynne poured herself a mug and pulled her favorite chair near the window to look out at the ocean. 'I've never felt this much peace.' She knew her life was blessed, rich in ways that few souls ever experience.

Turning her head to look at Cassy's photo she noticed something white under it. Reaching over she touched it. It felt warm as she pulled it from under the photo. It was folded in fourths; she quickly opened it and read: "*Deer, I'm so sorry...I can't stay. You're as beautiful as I've ever seen you. My own heart forever—My Deer*"

Lynne held the note close to her chest. Tears filled her eyes and ran. He always said she had the graceful legs of a deer. Only Lee called her 'deer' and spelled it that way.

'Oh Lee, my only love...'

Mason Haven

About six weeks after Sally and Amos's wedding Lisa woke with a feeling of slight nausea. 'Oops'—she thought, 'I'm late, what if!'

"The walk on the beach!" She said it right out loud to herself then dialed her doctor and made an appointment for the following Tuesday. When the exam was over he said,

"Alright Mrs. Mason" he said smiling, "you may get dressed and come into my office. I have some news for you."

The minute John came in from work that evening Lisa simply went to him, wrapped her arms around him and said,

"John I love you, and we are pregnant!"

"No," he said smiling—"really?"

"Really," she said, "and you love me very much," Lisa said with a wink.

"Fantastic, and I caught that remark"—he said grinning. "Hope you're as ready for another little one as I am."

"Oh yes I am John, so happy to be having another of your babies."

The following May 17th 1991 on Friday, Lisa gave birth to a son. She named him John Elliot Mason. He was a healthy whopping 9lbs. 2 oz. and 21 inches long. The whole family was thrilled with this new little person including Aunt Sally, and Uncle Amos. There would be many children for all of them to play with. Sally and Amos were also expecting their first baby! Lisa's new baby boy looked like John, and had his deep blue eyes!

"I'm curious Lisa," John said, "why'd you choose the name—Elliot?"

She said "well John he was conceived at *Berry Cove,* and that nice lady's name is Mrs. Elliot!"

"Oh," said John!

The Beginning…

0-595-25353-9